THE
TRAIN JUMPER

THE
TRAIN JUMPER

DON BROWN

A DEBORAH BRODIE BOOK
ROARING BROOK PRESS
NEW YORK

Text copyright © 2007 by Don Brown

A Deborah Brodie Book
Published by Roaring Brook Press
Roaring Brook Press is a division of
Holtzbrinck Publishing Holdings Limited Partnership
175 Fifth Avenue, New York, New York 10010
www.roaringbrookpress.com

Distributed in Canada by H. B. Fenn and Company, Ltd.

Library of Congress Cataloging-in-Publication Data
Brown, Don.
The train jumper / Don Brown.
p. cm.
Summary: Jumping freight trains during the Great Depression leads fourteen-year-old
Collie to a friendship with men and boys on their way to "somewhere else."
ISBN-13: 978-1-59643-218-5
ISBN-10: 1-59643-218-7
1. Depressions—1929—United States—Juvenile fiction. [1. Depressions—1929—
Fiction. 2. Poverty—Fiction. 3. Tramps—Fiction.] I. Title.
PZ7.B81297Tr 2007
[Fic]—dc22   2007003440

Roaring Brook Press books are available for special promotions and premiums. For
details, contact: Director of Special Markets, Holtzbrinck Publishers.

Book design by Jennifer Browne
Printed in the United States of America
First edition August 2007
2 4 6 8 10 9 7 5 3 1

For my wife, Deborah

A train.

Gray smoke plumed from the locomotive. It rolled past, making a clattering, hissing, chugging racket.

I bounced on the balls of my feet. Boxcars followed, one after another, worn-out things painted dull brown, gray, and green, many with their side doors wide open. I spotted a likely one and darted after it, stumbling in the cinders. The boxcar's grinding wheels sounded like knives being sharpened. I came to the open boxcar door.

Jump!

But I didn't.

Couldn't?

I kept running. My legs tired and my lungs burned.

Trains don't have legs and lungs, and they never tire. It kept *clack-clack-clack*ing forward, never slowing. The open boxcar pulled away. My chance was running away from me. With my last strength, I threw myself onto the train.

Only half of me made it.

My head and chest slammed onto the rough wood floor while my legs dangled from the opening. I was sure the train wheels were tickling my feet, and the thought of slipping beneath the train made my guts clench. I clawed the floor with my hands. Splinters stung my fingertips. But I felt myself sliding out. For an instant, I saw myself dropping beneath the train. Saw myself sliced in two.

I clawed harder.

Then hands grabbed my shirt and the seat of my pants and threw me into the boxcar like a sack of potatoes.

"Grab fer the handrails the next time, ya *idgit*," a voice said.

A scarecrow looked down at me, a tall, gray-haired man so skinny it looked as if his shabby shirt and pants were filled with sticks and not arms and legs.

"Thanks," I mumbled.

I caught my breath and rubbed the splinters from my fingers.

Scarecrow ambled to a corner of the boxcar, asking, "Ya got any grub?"

I thought the man was offering me food but quickly realized it was just the opposite.

"A couple of apples," I said.

The man held up his hands. I reached into my bag and tossed him one. He bit into it quickly.

"Where are you going?" I asked.

"The same place yer going," Scarecrow said. "Somewhere else."

Six years ago, in 1928, Dad had gone to work at the lumberyard like he did every day, except this time a truckload of logs rolled onto him, killing him dead in a blink. I was just eight at the time. There was lots of crying from me, Mom, and my older brother. And then, more bad stuff happened, one thing after the other, each rolling down on us like those logs off that truck.

Dad's paycheck from the lumberyard ended when he did, so Mom took a job at the electric pump factory doing something in the sales office, but it didn't pay as good as Dad's job had, and money was tight. Mom yanked us out of the house I'd been born in and moved us into a smaller place. The faucets dripped, and the seams of the flowered wallpaper didn't line up. Me and Little Bill shared a bedroom.

Little Bill is my older brother. He and Dad had the same name, so people called them Big and Little Bill to keep from confusing everybody. They kept calling him Little Bill even after Dad died. Habit, I guess.

To everybody I was Edward, Ed, or Eddy. I hated them all. I liked Collie, the nickname my pal Davy made out of my last name, Collier.

The next year, in 1929, the stock market crashed. I don't know how a bunch of rich guys going bust in New York City should make a difference in Wisconsin, but it did. The Crash shut down the pump factory, shut down factories and shops all over the country. Mom lost her job just like everyone else.

But she got lucky and found a part-time drugstore job, if, by lucky, you mean working for less than at the crummy pump factory.

Then Mom lost the drugstore job. No business, her boss explained, and he let her go. Our grocery tab got a lot longer, and the electric company shut off the lights. *In arrears*, they said, which is a fancy way of saying we didn't pay the bill.

Little Bill decided to quit school. After a few hours of standing in line with two hundred people waiting to fill fifty jobs at the newly reopened pump factory, he got to meet the guy doing the hiring, and it turned out to be an old pal of Dad's. The two had worked together years ago in the northern Wis- consin forests. When the guy found out Little Bill was the son of his old lumberjacking buddy, he hired Little Bill right off.

"You favor your old man," the guy told Little Bill, which he did.

Dad was a big guy with thick arms and giant shoulders. Little Bill was cut from the same pattern, except bigger. If Dad had lived, he would have had to look up at his son.

"You could swing a mean ax," the guy told Little Bill.

He would never have said that about me. I wasn't anything like Dad, favoring Mom instead: slight, slim, and with her straw-colored hair, too.

Little Bill going to work turned out to be another log of bad luck, but it didn't start out that way.

Little Bill's paycheck brought the lights back on. We ate good. Mom smiled more than she had since Dad died. And Little Bill was as sunny as a June day.

"Come on, Collie, get behind the wheel!" he'd said one Sunday after I'd helped him wash Dad's old Hudson.

"You pulling my leg?" I asked. I'd never driven before. He shook his head, grinning, and I climbed into the driver's seat.

"Here's the skinny. The buggy's got three speeds, and ya gotta push the gear shift in the right spot," he said, and with the engine off, he showed me where first, second, and third gear was. "But the only way to change gears is by pushing the clutch down with your foot. Give it a shot."

I worked the gears and clutch like he said.

"Here's the tough part," Little Bill explained. "As you let the clutch up, ya gotta give the engine some gas. Not too much and not too little. Just the right amount so the gears meet smooth. Then you can get going."

"How much is just right?" I asked.

"Can't really explain it. You just have to get a feel for it," he answered.

Getting the *feel* was no easy trick. I felt like a dumbbell. I stalled the engine again and again. The car lurched and staggered as I tried to get it rolling. But Little Bill didn't care. He squealed and giggled at every wobble and reel, like we were on a carnival ride.

After flubbing it again, I pounded the steering wheel and yelled, "What am I doing wrong?"

"Don't get your bowels in an uproar. Start her up again," Little Bill said. "Put her into first. Okay. Now let the clutch up. *Slowly.* Yeah, that's it. Give it some gas. *Too much.* Better. Keep the clutch going. And gas. That's it. That's it. *That's it!*"

We were rolling!

The two of us started laughing, and I forgot to steer. Little Bill had to yank the wheel and drive us around a parked car.

We went around the block a half-dozen times, laughing like hyenas the whole time, before Little Bill called it quits. Getting out of the car, he threw his arm around me.

"When can we do it again?" I asked.

"Sometime," he said.

But we never did.

One night after work, Little Bill came home stinking drunk.

He'd visited a saloon with a bunch of factory guys. He got drunk another night, and then another. Pretty soon, he showed up burping beer and talking loud all the time. Then he'd grab me for a wrestling match, which was less wrestling than him just bending arms and legs until I screamed.

"Aw, ya crybaby," he'd laugh, and Mom would have to slap him off me.

Mom finally blew up and they had an awful fight. Mom

told Little Bill that it wasn't right for him to be drinking at seventeen. Wasn't right to hurt me. But Little Bill just screamed, "As long as I make the money, I'll do what I want!"

Mom sagged and stopped nagging him about the boozing.

After that, he went to work during the day and drank with his buddies at night. And I guessed things would have gone on like that forever if the workers at the factory hadn't called a strike.

"It's a freaking crime, taking advantage of tough times and expecting us to work for next to nothing," Little Bill explained.

He was probably right. But the strikers hadn't figured on a whole crop of other people who didn't give a hoot about low pay or strikes and were happy to have any kind of work. The factory hired them and dumped the strikers.

"Freaking scabs! Foreigners!" Little Bill spat, banging his fist onto the kitchen table. But I heard most everybody hired was local.

Little Bill came home soused that night, kicking open the door and screaming at Mom to make him a sandwich. She explained, "There's no bread, William."

He slapped the wall and stomped around the kitchen, cursing.

"It's late, Little Bill. Why don't you go to bed?" I said, trying to calm him down.

He grabbed my shirt with both fists.

"Don't ever tell me what to do!" he shouted, pushing his face close to mine.

"William!" Mom cried.

"Crybaby," he hissed, and tossed me like a rag to the floor.

One day, while throwing a ball in the air, I noticed our neighbor, Mr. Custer, struggling to tie a ladder to the roof of his old car. I gave him a hand lashing it down and helped him load the trunk with buckets and boxes.

"I'm painting a house for some extra dough. Ya wanna help? I'll pay ya," he said.

Eager to make some money, too, I hopped into the car and we headed off before I even had the chance to tell Mom. Afterward, he flipped me a buck!

"Edward!" Mom cried when I came home paint-splattered. She was going to rip me for ruining my clothes, but I cut her short when I held up a chicken I'd bought at the market. I told her my good news.

"And I got some dough left over," I said, handing the coins to her.

"You're a sweetheart!" she gushed.

Little Bill came in, and Mom told him the good news.

"Isn't it wonderful Edward can help the family?" she asked.

He grunted.

A few days later, I helped Mr. Custer again, which meant another chicken dinner.

"We're proud of you, Edward," Mom said.

"Yeah, you're a regular little breadwinner," Little Bill said with a sneer as he chowed down on a drumstick.

Afterward, he went to the bar where he and his drinking buddies were still celebrating the end of Prohibition a year earlier. Drinking was legal again. He returned home soused and grabbed me for a wrestling match. I ended up on the floor, all twisted up.

"Say *Uncle*," he teased, squashing my nose down into the rug.

"*Uncle*," I squeaked.

"I can't hear you."

"*Uncle!*"

I was seeing stars when Mom found us and chased Little Bill off me.

"What a stinking mama's boy!" he said.

When I worked for Mr. Custer again, I gave all the money to Mom and didn't bother getting a chicken.

A few days later, I was leaving the house as Little Bill drove up. Getting out of the car, he said, "Ran into old man Custer. Knocked back some beers with him down at the Dew Drop. Asked me to give him a hand with the paint jobs. Going out on a job with him tomorrow."

He walked into the house. On fire, I chased him.

"You creep!" I shouted.

"Whadaya talking about?" he asked.

"My job! You stole my job!" I yelled.

"You don't know nothing about stolen jobs," he hissed, grabbing my arm and twisting. "Nothin'!"

He yanked my arm hard.

"My arm," I squeaked, turning myself so my shoulder would have a bit more give.

But he cranked it more, until electric pain shot from my elbow and I screamed.

After the sling came off, I was good as new, except when my pal Davy and I had a catch. My elbow stung when I threw. But it was no big deal, it wasn't like the Yankees were knocking down my door to join Babe Ruth and Lou Gehrig.

Little Bill didn't bother me much after that, other than calling me a dope or a mama's boy. But one night changed everything.

He came home on a bender, slamming the door open and stomping into the house.

"I had that friggin' job. I had it!" Little Bill bellowed, stalking back and forth like a caged leopard.

"Job?" Mom asked.

I guessed it was another chance for a job that ended in a dead end.

Little Bill didn't answer, instead slapped his hand flat against the battered kitchen table. Then he opened the icebox and rooted inside, clumsily knocking a bit of butter onto the floor. Slamming the icebox shut, he shouted, "Ain't there ever anything to eat?"

Mom bent to pick up the butter just as Little Bill

stumbled toward the cupboards. The two collided, sending Mom flying into the cabinets and crashing to the floor.

"Ma!" I cried.

She touched her finger to a bleeding lip.

Little Bill stared.

"It's nothing. Nothing. A bump. An accident," she said.

I grabbed a dish towel and handed it to her. She dabbed her lip, repeating, "It's nothing. Nothing."

I turned to glare at Little Bill, but he was gone.

Good riddance, I thought to myself. But after three days, he was still gone and Mom grew frantic.

"He's probably off on a bender," I told her. "Probably holed up with one of his drinking buddies."

"Yes. That must be it," she agreed, kneading her hands.

It was Mr. Custer who brought us the news that Little Bill had run off.

"Little Bill came by a few nights ago. Said he was gonna join the CCC. I figured he'd squared it with you, otherwise I woulda told you right away," he explained to Mom and me.

"The CCC?" I asked.

"Yeah. Civilian Conservation Corps. Something Roosevelt came up with. Hires young guys to cut roads, clear trees, fight fires. Take care of the land. Kinda like an army of lumberjacks. Little Bill got all jazzed up talking about it."

"Where is it?"

"They got camps all over. Little Bill said something about a Colorado camp north of Grand Junction."

Mom shrank at the news.

I tried to comfort her and said, "I'll get work. I'm four-teen. Just about the age Little Bill started at the factory. I'll take care of us. We'll get by."

"It's not about money, Edward. It's losing William. He's ashamed and stubborn. He'll never come back. He's gone. First your father and now him. The family's breaking like a shattered plate," she said, and cried and cried.

That's when I decided to find him and bring him home.

Scarecrow finished the apple. Night fell and he went to sleep. I watched house lights twinkle in the distance for a long time, until I fell asleep, too.

I awoke in the morning. The train had stopped. The summer air was soft and warm. A shaft of pancake-colored light beamed through the freight's open door. Scarecrow stood there, spying out.

"The bulls got a darkie," Scarecrow whispered.

I peeked out.

Two large white men pinned a colored man against the side of a boxcar and smacked his head with a large flashlight.

"Nobody rides my railroad without a ticket! Ya hear that, boy?" one man grunted as he swung the flashlight again and again. "Ya hear that, boy?"

"The bulls will be busy with the darkie for a piece. Chance to beat it," Scarecrow laughed, lifting a canvas sack.

He leaped out of the boxcar and sprinted into the brush.

Being left alone so suddenly made my heart race. I saw the colored man curled on the ground, holding his head and rocking back and forth. One of the white men pawed inside a tattered suitcase, spilling its contents over the cinders.

"Ya got any cash, boy?" the bull growled, while his partner stood to one side, a revolver held loosely in his hand.

A dozen hobos leaped from the other boxcars in ones and twos and dashed into the woods. Not knowing what else to do, I snatched up my bag, took an enormous gulp of air, and hightailed it into the weeds.

"Hey!" someone shouted.

I crawled through thick brush until the earth suddenly fell away and I slid into a stinking drainage ditch. Scrambling to my feet, I ran through trees. Small branches slapped my arms and face. I skidded to a halt at a large, grassy field flowered in the haze of a zillion flying bugs.

I saw men. Bulls with flashlights and revolvers? I threw myself flat and peeked out. A shabby lot of teenagers, young men, and a few gray-heads milled about a trashy campground. Damp clothes dried on low bushes, there for the want of a line. A small hand mirror dangled from a branch, reflecting the sudsy face of someone shaving. Sacks and suitcases, all the worse from wear, dotted the camp, companions to men and boys stretched or standing beside them.

Like a late-arriving passenger's at a bus stop, my showing up excited no one. A few heads turned toward me, measured me for a moment, and then turned away. Scarecrow was there, staring at a simmering stew pot. Ribbons of steam drifted up, tickling my nose with promises of meat and gravy. My empty stomach did somersaults.

Scarecrow noticed me staring at the pot and said, "Mulligan stew. Ya can take some if ya add some. Throw in a potato or some carrots. Then you'll be able to take a dip."

Two hobos came to the pot and dropped in turnips and celery. Scarecrow produced a potato from his sack and added it to the stew.

Get yourself a potato? Why didn't he just tell me to get myself a diamond stick pin.

I turned away, the bubbling pot too much of a torture to stay near to.

"Ah, hell," Scarecrow muttered. "Here."

He tossed me a potato.

"That's fer the apple last night, so don't go thanking me. We're even now," he explained. "Go ahead and drop 'er in."

I slid it into the simmering stew and took a seat alongside a dozen others circling the pot as if it were some kind of god.

The minutes dragged like they were crippled before the stew was cooked and plates and tins and spoons appeared from backpacks, suitcases, and bedrolls. Soon, everyone was eating.

"Go ahead, boy. Take yer share. It's yer right," Scarecrow muttered to me. "Geez, ya ain't got a tin?"

He dug a canteen cup and a spoon from his sack and

handed them to me, saying, "That's jus' a borrow. I want 'em back."

I ladled out a full portion of stew. At the end, I cleaned the dregs with my fingers, licking them so clean afterward that they were as shiny and pink as a baby's.

I tried to sleep. People joking, whispering, snoring, and farting made for a restless night. When the sun rose I was still dog tired. Heading wearily back to the tracks, it struck me that I was miles from home with only the foggiest idea of how to find Little Bill.

I discovered Scarecrow standing in the railroad cinders.

"Train coming?" I asked.

"Sooner or later," Scarecrow said, and our conversation went dead.

I remembered the green apple and pulled it from my bag. He gave me a sideways glance. Suddenly his face lit up. Pointing toward the weeds, he said, "Hey, over there."

A small battered suitcase rested in the bushes behind me, the one that belonged to the colored guy grabbed by the bulls.

"Take it. The darkie won't be needing it anymore," Scarecrow said.

"It's not empty," I said.

"Fifty-fifty split," he said quickly.

"What about the colored guy?" I asked, but Scarecrow

ignored me and divvied up the fella's belongings. Scarecrow got two pairs of socks, a sweater, and a tweed cap. I got a bar of soap, a T-shirt, and a pair of pants.

"Look," I said, pulling a pocket watch from the pants pocket.

"Give it here," Scarecrow said, and stuffed it in his pocket.

Didn't seem even-steven to me, but I kept my yap shut.

Scarecrow looked down the empty rails and asked, "Don't think a freight is coming soon. Ya wanna head to the main stem and angle for an odd job?"

I double-checked for a train and nodded. Little Bill would have to wait.

On Main Street, Scarecrow nosed around for work.

"Ya want your walk sweeped?" Scarecrow asked, or "Them boxes need lifting? Want them windows washed? Hole dug? Door fixed? Trash removed?"

But nobody wanted nothing. The noonday sun was high and hot. We stood outside a swell house with a wraparound porch, and Scarecrow said, "This place is a good one. Ya see, the paint ain't half bad, the car in the driveway's been washed, even got decent tires. Hard times ain't wearing these people down."

I wanted to head back to the tracks.

"Knock on the door. Give it a shot," Scarecrow said.

"Are you nuts? I'm not gonna ask a stranger for work!" I said, my stomach flip-flopping at the thought of it.

"Don't be a sap. You got a better chance than an old moocher like me," he explained, pushing me to the back door. "Tell 'em their lawn needs a haircut. Tell 'em we'll do the job for fifty cents. *Fifty cents*, ya hear me?"

He shooed me toward the front door. I knocked, and a balloon-faced woman with the down-turned lips of a person who has stepped in dog flop answered. I stammered the yard work deal to her, and she agreed. Then she closed the door on my nose.

We mowed and raked and swept the grass for three hours.

"Get the dough," Scarecrow said when we finished.

"The bushes aren't trimmed," said the woman when I tried to collect.

"Ma'am, you said all we had to do was mow the lawn. Well, we did that and raked and—"

"Don't try and pull a fast one on me. I wasn't born yesterday. I said to trim the bushes, and if you don't want to, well, then all you'll get is air. The clippers are in the garage," she argued, stroking her pearl necklace.

"Holy mackerel!" Scarecrow spit when I gave him the news, but we got the clippers.

A half hour later, I tapped on the kitchen door again, announcing, "Bushes are done, Ma'am."

The woman pulled coins from her purse and dropped four dimes into my hand.

"Um, Ma'am, you promised fifty cents," he said.

"Fifty cents for a decent job. Not the shoddy work of you and your friend."

"But—"

"Shoddy."

"We mowed and raked and—"

"Ethel!" a voice interrupted. It was a cigar-stained voice, and I guessed it was her husband.

"What now?" she muttered, strutting away.

Their voices carried back to me. It sounded like bickering. Glancing around the kitchen, I noticed the remains of a large meal: roast beef, carrots, red potatoes in gravy, and biscuits bigger than your hand. The platters spilled food.

The two voices in the nearby room, one grating, the other rasping, continued like bolts shaken in a tin cup. The moments dragged. I shifted my weight from one foot to the other.

"Geez, are they gonna gab forever?" I mumbled to myself.

What would Scarecrow say if I didn't get the fifty cents? My heart climbed into my throat. I bounced the dimes in my hand, and glanced at the door leading to the hallway. The voices of rattling bolts kept talking.

I looked at the dimes resting in my filthy, scratched palm. My thumbnail, which had been mashed against a tree limb, was yellow-purple.

"Fifty cents. We said *fifty* cents," I whispered.

The food attracted flies. The sight steamed me. I had as much right to eat as a bug!

I tiptoed to the counter, picked up a couple of slabs of beef and biscuits, and fashioned a couple of sandwiches. I convinced myself that two cuts of meat and a couple of biscuits were worth ten cents, and I hadn't stolen anything.

Dashing out the back door, I galloped around the house.

"Cheese it!" I shouted to Scarecrow, and he threw down the hedge shears and lit out after me.

We ate, and Scarecrow shared some tricks of the hobo trade. He said, "There's three ways you can get some dough. *One*, you can steal it. *Two*, you can beg for it. When you put the touch on a guy, you wanna check the shoes first. A guy might have a dirty job, and get his clothes filthy and fulla holes, well, that's just the way it is and he wears 'em. But only bums walk around with holes in their shoes. Remember: good shoes—put the arm on the guy, ask him if he can spare a dime. Rotten shoes—let'm pass 'cause he's no better off than you."

I nodded, but I'd never hit up a stranger for spare change. Begging just seemed too low down.

"What's the third way?" I asked.

"Work. Not J. P. Morgan work. Not white collars and soft hands work. Sweat work. Sweeping, stacking, cutting, piling, packing. Lifting and hauling. Digging and dragging. *Work*."

He treated me like a regular joe, and I decided to tell him about my plan on finding Little Bill, although I didn't level with him on why Little Bill had run away.

"Catching the right trains is the trick. Hoppin' a wrong one would mean a detour and wasted time. Could add days to the trip. But hobos along the way could help, could point out the route," Scarecrow said. He looked at his last bite of roast beef before popping it into his mouth. "Yup. It's all in the right jumps. We could do it."

We?

"You're coming?" I asked, and held my breath. I'd been dreading being on my own again and hopping trains with no idea of what I was doing.

"Why not? Ain't tramped out west. Couldn't be worse than here."

"That would be swell!"

"But, here's the deal. We gotta jump off along the way now and then, take a break and angle for food. I'm too old to ride a freight for days on an empty stomach."

"Deal!"

We shook hands. Before you could say "jack rabbit" we were beside the rails, watching an oncoming freight rumble toward us. The thundering locomotive rattled the air, shook the earth, and snorted steam and smoke like a monster in a fairy tale. Tank cars followed the engine, and then an endless line of boxcars. They appeared to stretch back to yesterday.

This was only my second catch-on. I shook the memory of the hash I'd made of my first time and tried to pick a likely looking boxcar. I was about to chase one when Scarecrow pressed his hand to my chest.

"Listen, you don't just run willy-nilly after a freight. That's a good way to get yourself killed," he said. "And being run down by a train ain't pretty, let me tell you. They gotta bury you in pieces. So use your head.

"First you gotta decide if you're fast enough. You gotta figure that out on your own. Everybody's different, you see. Me, I can kick it up to a pretty good run. Don't have the slightest idea about you. Maybe you're a turtle, maybe you're a hare.

"If you think the train is going too fast, then it probably is, and then it's plain stupid to chase it. You'll just run out of breath, legs'll get weak, maybe you stumble, and the next thing you know, you're rolling under the wheels and it's curtains for you.

"If you think you're fast enough, then you gotta decide where you're gonna hop on. If it's the side door, you want to grab hold of the frame or the handrail, if it's got one. Then you have to go whole hog, throw yourself in without being iffy about it. Otherwise you'll end up half in and half out like you did when I grabbed you. Who knows what would have happened if I hadn't fished you in.

"If you try for the rungs at the back of the car and miss, there's a good chance you'll stumble into the space between cars where the coupling is. Fall there and you can count on going into the wheels. Like throwing yourself into a meat grinder.

"Got it?"

I nodded. He pushed me forward. I sprinted after an open door, grabbed the frame, and threw myself in. Easy as pie. He followed me in. I smiled but he didn't congratulate me or nothing. I guess not getting killed was my reward. Congratulations or not, I didn't care. I was on my way.

He told me to call him Hack, which I did, but I never thought of him as anything other than Scarecrow. The only thing I'd learned about him was that he was from southern Missouri, and his granddaddy had fought with Hood during the War Between the States.

"You always been a hobo?"

Scarecrow said, "Naa, but it feels like it. You'll understand soon enough."

We rode a few short hops, stopping in between to angle for food. The trains were jammed with tramps and hobos, and you'd have to climb to the catwalk and ride on the boxcar roof. There were times when so many people huddled in the cars, loafed on the catwalks, and even hung from the rods *beneath* the cars, that I wondered if everybody in the whole country was on the move. One long freight had boxcars that snaked all the way back to the horizon, and had hundreds of hobos sprinkled across the top like jimmies on an ice cream cone.

Mostly it was teenagers or young men, although there were a fair number of older guys like Scarecrow. We shared a boxcar with a couple of teenage girls once, it coming as a shock. They'd caught-on after dark, each in bulky jackets and caps. I figured them for a couple of boys and didn't learn different until the next morning, when their long hair fell out of their caps.

Nights were spent in jungles, hobo camps, and around the mulligan stew pot, gossiping about other tramps, trains, and bulls.

I learned about the different lines. The Union Pacific, the B&O, the Santa Fe, Northen Pacific, and a million feeder lines connecting one jerkwater town to another. Hobos knew lines the way regular folks knew which street to take to the grocery store.

But it was the trains that really got hobos' blood pumping. They loved talking about them, and knew them better than a cow knows its calf. Knew 'em right down to their bolts, and could throw around words like *blast pipe*, *ash box hopper*, and *rear bogle* like they'd designed 'em themselves. They knew the train names too: Super Chief, Crow Flyer, Twentieth Century.

I once listened for an hour about a four-six-four, a locomotive with four front wheels, six middle traction wheels, and four rear wheels. Four-six-fours pulled passenger trains faster than a scream.

"Rode the blinds behind a four-six-four pulling the Crow Flyer down in Arkansas. Stupidest stunt I ever pulled," a hobo joked, and everyone laughed knowingly.

"What are the blinds?" I later asked Scarecrow.

"Platform at the end door of a passenger train's baggage car. Stuff's all piled up at the door, so nobody's gonna open 'er up and find you riding there," he explained.

"Why don't we ride the blinds? Passenger trains gotta be faster than the slow freights we've been catching on."

"You ain't ready, kid. Riding the blinds is like hanging on to the back of a car, standing on the bumper, and then shooting the car out of a cannon. A four-six-four flies along at seventy, eighty, ninety miles an hour! And a four-six-four don't care if you're tired, or cold, or wet, or hungry, or crying for your mama. Once it gets going, it might not stop for ten hours. No, kid, you ain't ready for that."

We short-hopped from town to town, days passed, and I itched to *get going*.

"Gotta find a hobo who can point us to the right line," Scarecrow explained when I groused.

But we never seemed to find the right hobo. Instead we'd be angling for jobs, or I should say, I angled for jobs. It seems I had the knack for it and could land us work out of the blue.

"It's the puppy dog in ya. People can't bear to turn you away," Scarecrow laughed. "You're 'Pup' from here on out."

The craziest job was washing fat pink Dolley Madison. Dolley Madison was a big old sow.

"She got to be pretty for the fair," said the woman who owned her as we sudsed up the pig. Cleaning that sow was like washing a car on the deck of a steamship in a storm. Ol' Dolley would tiptoe this way and that, and there was no stopping her. I think me and Scarecrow got as much soap on us as on her. The woman gave us eight bits for the job, and having the dough in my pocket was better than being broke, soapy or not.

Afterward, we stopped at a restaurant. *Flynt's Fine Dining*, the sign read. Scarecrow said, "Thought for once we could celebrate our good fortune."

The thought of having a sit-down dinner made me giddy. But when I got inside I discovered the place was a gin joint. I thought about the problems drinking had made for Little Bill and me. It wasn't the place I would have picked.

The joint was jumpin' and there were a lot of people. People talked loud and horselaughed. A cloud of cigarette smoke drifted like a fog.

"Whadaya havin'?" a waitress asked.

"Two beers," Scarecrow said, smiling.

"One beer," I corrected.

"*Two* beers," Scarecrow said, glancing at me and adding, "They're both for me."

"A two-fisted drinker, hey, cowboy?" the waitress joked, turning toward the bar.

"And a hard-boiled egg," he called after her.

"Help yourself," she replied.

Scarecrow rose and plucked an egg from a giant glass jar filled with them. He sat back down, peeled off the shell, and bit off the top.

"Ain't ya gonna eat?" he asked.

"That's it, hard-boiled eggs?" I asked. "There's nothing else?"

"That's pretty much the long and the short of it. They

cook a mess of eggs soze they can call themselves a restaurant," he answered.

The waitress returned with two tall beers. Scarecrow finished one with a long slug.

"There anything else to eat other than hard-boiled eggs?" I asked the waitress.

"We serve spaghetti and meatballs on Fridays," she said.

It was Tuesday.

"What am I supposed to do, just sit here and watch you get plastered?" I asked.

Scarecrow shrugged.

"Geez, I'll meet you back here in an hour," I said.

Wandering around, I came to a field and a bunch of guys my age playing ball. They played a swell ball game with a rubber ball and a broomstick, three to a side. One guy pitched, and the other two stayed in the outfield. There wasn't any base running or nothing. Bases were scored by how far the fly balls landed.

One kid ran for a ball and tripped, bloodying his nose. His pals laughed and told him to sit out for a minute.

"Hey, mack, ya wanna play some ball? We need another guy," a player called to me, a beefy blond kid.

"Thanks, but I gotta get going," I said. I had to get back to Scarecrow.

When I got to the saloon, a colored man was throwing him out by the scruff of his neck.

"Watch it, you dumb drunk!" said the colored man, pushing Scarecrow away.

"Lemme alone!" Scarecrow grunted. "Darkie!"

The colored man, a big-shouldered guy, swatted Scarecrow's head, knocking him into the gutter.

"Don't push me, cracker!" the colored man said, pointing a finger at Scarecrow.

I raced between them, saying, "I got 'im, mister. I'll get him outa here."

"Make sure he doesn't come back. The boss don't want troublemakers here, especially the low-down type like him."

I got Scarecrow to his feet, and we stumbled back to the jungle. He fell on his things and started snoring. Him getting stinking drunk burned me up, and I hardly slept. All kinds of things bounced around my head like balls in a bingo drum. I heard a clock tick inside my head, reminding me that Mom was waiting for me while I wasted time angling for odd jobs. Angling for odd jobs *for Scarecrow*! I started to think that maybe Scarecrow was confusing me with the goose that laid the golden egg. I told him so, too, the next morning.

"I ain't your meal ticket!" I said. I was sure he was hung over and feeling miserable, because I'd seen the same look on Little Bill after he'd slept off a drunk.

Calling me his meal ticket must have struck a nerve because he got red and said, "Okay, okay. We'll make better time. I promise."

He dragged himself to his feet, rubbed his eyes, and we headed to the rails, where we were lucky to find a freight just passing.

We rode the catwalk, the centerboard running the length of a boxcar roof. It wasn't a hard trick as long as the train was moving slow and the bounces and bumps were small. I wouldn't have wanted to try it if we were barreling along.

The train clattered and clinked. Scarecrow felt good enough to stand up on the catwalk and let his legs absorb the jigs and bounces of the ride.

"What gives?" I asked when the train slowed.

"Engine probably needs water," he replied, and we climbed down into the boxcar to wait.

The freight shuddered to a stop, and boxcars clanged together. Suddenly, a colored boy jumped into our boxcar. He was bigger and thicker than me. A tattered cap covered short hair. He stepped back in surprise, nearly tripping over his boots, beat-up brown things that had no laces. He pulled the stained sack he carried tight to himself.

"Car's full, boy," Scarecrow said. "Move on."

The boy looked around the empty boxcar. He narrowed his black-brown eyes and balled one hand into a fist.

"Move on, boy," Scarecrow said, his voice sharper. "Not sharing a car with a jig."

The boy sneered, then hopped out.

The train started up again and rolled to a scruffy town cowering beside silent, shuttered lumber mills, where the train stopped. Stuck for the night, there wasn't anything else to do but look for work. All we got was the high hat.

"Hit the bricks, ya bum. Nobody's givin' me a handout!" one man barked.

We found a jungle and watched others eat mulligan stew. One of them was the colored kid we'd seen earlier. The kid spooned soup and gave us the evil eye.

There wasn't a freight the next day. But we had better luck at scrounging around for food and were able to add a little something to the stew pot. I noticed the colored kid sitting off to the side, not eating. I guess it was his turn to go hungry. Our eyes met, and he glared.

Scarecrow swallowed some stew and said, "Tomorrow will be the charm. Got a feeling. Train'll come and we'll be on our way. You'll see. Be meeting up with that brother of yours in no time."

Scarecrow was right about the train. But it didn't take me to Little Bill.

"**A**w, Geez!" Scarecrow grunted, waking me. "We're in the yard."

"A yard?" I mumbled, wiping sleep from my eyes.

"The railroad yard. Where they hook and unhook the cars. Where the bulls are. Get caught in the yards and it's a busted head for sure."

He swept his things together and crawled to the door. My heart racing, I followed. But as I scrambled toward him, he shooed me away, whispering, "There's a bunch of railroad hands uncoupling cars nearby."

We scuttled to the other door. Looking up and down the rails, Scarecrow said, "Nobody. Let's go."

We dropped to the cinders and kneeled beside the train wheels. The voices of railroad mugs got closer. I remembered the bull smacking the colored guy, and my stomach did somersaults. Scarecrow pointed to a line of cattle cars nearby, and we ran.

Ducking between two cars, we jumped to the ladders leading up to the catwalk and pressed ourselves flat. I held my breath and peeked out. Railroad workers climbed into our old boxcar.

"Weeee-OOOOOOO!"

The sudden train whistle surprised me, and I nearly fell off the ladder. The cows made an awful racket of lowing as I recovered my grip. Then the car shuddered, and loud clangs ran the length of the freight as couplings banged tight together. We started rolling—back in the direction we'd just come!

The idea of heading off the wrong way and wasting more time made me crazy.

"We gotta get off!" I shouted to Scarecrow over the noisy cows.

He shook his head and yelled something I couldn't hear.

The freight gathered speed. If we didn't get off soon, it would be too late.

"I'm going!" I hollered.

Scarecrow reached for me, but I brushed him away. I tossed my suitcase and leaped after it. Tumbling into the cinders, I belly-skidded to a stop and a dust cloud billowed around me. Dirt filled my mouth and eyes, and I coughed and cried dusty tears as I got to my knees. Suddenly, something swatted me back down and stars danced before me.

"Nobody rides my railroad without a ticket," a voice growled.

I was lifted up and brought face-to-face with a giant bull. I tried squirming away but he just gathered the folds of my collar into his ham-hock mitt until the material choked me like a noose. He growled, "Where do you think yer going, ya miserable little mug?"

He dragged me away as easily as a cat drags a sparrow, kicking my stuff onto the rails.

"You won't be needing that where you're going," he muttered.

The judge gave me thirty days. "Vagrancy," he said. I asked him what vagrancy was.

"Mean's you're broke," he said.

"I ain't broke. I had nearly two bucks but the bull took it from me!" I cried.

After the bull had caught me, he'd taken me to a railroad shed.

"You think you can ride the railroad without a ticket, do you?" he'd said, and slapped me hard. "Do ya?"

"Geez, I got money! I'll pay for the ride. I'll pay!" I cried.

"Yeah, I bet. Let's see," he said.

I dug coins out of my pocket and handed them over. But it didn't go for no railroad ticket. Instead, he stuffed the dough into his pockets and then hauled me off to a cop waiting outside the yard.

"Here's some trash for ya," he said, and gave the back of my head another smack.

The cop took me to a courthouse, a small building with marble pillars that held up the roof, except they weren't marble, because wood peeked out of the bare spots in the paint. Inside, the judge, a bald guy in a wrinkled suit and unbuttoned shirt collar, asked me a bunch of questions. What had I done? Why was I there? Was I alone? I tried to tell him about finding Little Bill, but he told me to shut up.

"Thirty days," he said, and that was that.

The cop brought me to a bench outside the courtroom and said, "Don't move. Or else."

I stayed glued to the bench for hours. I hoped Scarecrow would show up, which was an awful thought because it would mean he was in the same jam as me. But he never did, and I guess he stayed on the cattle car and was miles away by now. The judge's sentence bounced around inside my head. *Thirty days!* Finding Little Bill seemed like a million years away. Slumping against the wall, I fell asleep. The cop's hand woke me as he hooked my armpit and lifted me.

"Where we going?" I asked.

"Shaddup," he muttered.

He brought me outside and to a waiting green Packard.

Leaning into the side window, he said, "He's all yours now."

He pushed me into the backseat. Sitting there was the colored kid that Scarecrow had chased out of our boxcar days earlier.

He glared at me with the same evil eye he'd given me at the jungle. The Packard drove away. The driver, a goofy-looking character with a shaved head and the turned-forward ear of a pig, never said a word. He took us to a storefront. "Spearmint Street Mission" was painted across its window.

"Let's go," said Pig Ears, and me and the colored kid followed him through a back door and into a large room with benches and tables. The place overflowed with people, mostly men, family guys, old timers, hobos, kids like me, dressed in duds and rags, but there were women and girls, too, just not as many. Everybody was squashed together at the long tables, talking, laughing, arguing, muttering, crying, babbling, sobbing, and snorting over bowls of soup. I slowed down to look but got shoved from behind by the colored kid. We squirmed through the crowd and followed Pig Ears through a doorway and into a small kitchen.

A half-dozen people stirred pots on a large black stove, cleaned potatoes, and washed bowls in a basin of dirty water. The steaming soup, frantic action, and low ceiling heated the room. A man with a sack of potatoes in each arm strode in. The sacks were big, but it was nothing for the man; he was huge, even bigger than Little Bill.

"Sweet Lord, it's hot in here. Leave the darn door open!" he roared, dropping the sacks. Spying me and the colored kid, he asked, "These our new recruits?"

"Yup. They got pulled off a Southern Pacific freight," Pig Ears said.

"Just two?"

"Four others went to the Salvation Army."

"Of course they get the lion's share. Got the name. The reputation."

Pig Ears nodded.

"And I bet these two are the runts of the litter," the man said.

Another nod.

The man sighed.

"Boys, welcome to the Spearmint Street Mission. You'll be helping us here for the next thirty days. And I do mean the whole thirty days. Ya try to take a powder, I promise we'll find you and bring you back, except you won't come here but to the County Lockup, where you'll do the remainder of your time plus another thirty. And believe me, it's a sight better here than working a chain gang fixing roads. A sight better!

"Take heart, boys. You'll be doing the Lord's work here. But even though it's the Lord's work, you'll be answering to me. I'm Pastor Lester X. Wryte. Folks call me Papa Bear."

☞

Papa Bear told Pig Ears to give us the "lay of the land," and we followed him on a tour of the mission.

"This here is the back door, where the unfortunates line up for soup. And once they're in, the door is locked up for the night. This here door is locked and opened only by me," he said between phlegmy coughs.

He led us back to the kitchen and said, "This here kitchen is the food cooking place and the dish cleaning place. You guys will be working here."

"What will we be doing?" I asked.

"Cooking food and cleaning dishes, what did ya think?" he answered.

"But—" I started to say.

"But nothing! It's your job to shut up and do as you're told," he said, and the colored kid grinned at my tongue-lashing.

We entered the large front room, which had rows of benches before a wooden platform. Pig Ears said, "This here is the Sermon Room. The Chapel. Papa Bear gives his sermons here and saves souls. If you catch somebody napping through a sermon, you gotta give 'em a poke. If they keep dozing off, you gotta remind them that there ain't no meal without taking in the sermon."

"A fella don't get fed if he hasn't listened to the sermon? What if he comes in late?" I asked.

"Latecomers are turned away. Everybody around here knows the deal. The food don't cost nothing except some time with Papa Bear," he said, picking his nose.

We went back to the kitchen. People were cooking, and Pig Ears told us to pitch in.

Three hours later, I found myself mopping sweat from my forehead. The two bags that Papa Bear had so easily carried lay open at my feet. I grabbed a potato, peeled it with a dull knife, carving the eyes from it, shaving its skin until it was the size of a walnut, and dropping it into a giant pot of water.

Then I did it again.

And again.

The pot filled, and another one took its place. That one filled and was replaced.

No matter how many potatoes I cleaned, the bags never seemed to lighten. My knife hand cramped. I sighed.

Papa Bear came in and caught me taking a breather. He laughed. "You're doing the Lord's work. No goldbricking."

I reached for another potato.

The colored kid washed dishes. The pile of dirty bowls never got smaller. It was dinnertime, and there were a lot of hungry people, and the place needed lots of bowls. He must've thought I got the sweeter job, because the only looks he gave me were dirty ones.

Everybody who showed up got fed for free, no questions asked. I even saw a swell-dressed guy in a suit and a homburg join the soup line. All you had to do was hold out a bowl and in would go the soup. Then you'd grab a slice of bread and find a seat. You could even take seconds, but there was a sign on the wall that read *Save some for your brothers and sisters*, which kind of discouraged you from hogging the food.

Another sign read *Have you written your mother?* It made me sad because I hadn't, and I knew she was probably worried sick about me, no matter how well my friend Davy had explained stuff to her like I'd asked him to.

After supper, the soup eaters were herded to the front room. They all understood that the price of the dinner was listening to a sermon by Papa Bear. The sharpies who tried to sneak out found locked exits.

We stacked the dinner tables and threw blankets on the floor. When the sermon ended, the crowd trudged back and fell onto the blankets. People talked, laughed, whispered, and snored; it reminded me of the jungles.

Papa Bear found me and the colored kid and said, "Fine start, boys. Now find a blanket and get some rest. You'll need it."

"We didn't eat," said the colored kid. It was the first time I heard him speak.

"Can't have a couple of good workers go hungry, can we? Make a sandwich from anything you find in the icebox," he said, and headed out.

Me and the colored kid walked into the empty kitchen. When the door closed behind us, he flew at me, bowled me over, and ended up on top of me with one of his hands clamped around my neck.

"What—!" I gurgled.

"That pal 'a yours, that redneck, stole from me! Ya understand? He stole from me!" he snarled.

"What did he steal?" I gasped.

"My socks! He stole my socks and I only got one extra pair! Saw him do it, saw it with my own eyes. Snuck into my stuff when he thought the jungle was empty. You a part of that? He give them socks to you?"

"No. I'm no thief," I croaked.

He waved his fist in front of my nose.

"I'm telling you, I'm no thief!" I said, finally tearing his hand from my throat.

He unfolded his fist and got off me.

Cool as a cucumber, he made himself a sandwich. I stood.

Papa Bear came into the kitchen and said, "After you fill your bellies, get some sleep."

He patted my shoulder and smiled. After being jumped by the colored kid, the friendly gesture was like getting a Christmas present.

"Sure thing! Thanks!" I said, and before I knew it, the story poured out of me about . . . everything!

Papa Bear listened hard as I told him about Mom, Little Bill, Scarecrow, and the nasty setup by the railroad bull that had landed me in the clink. He stroked his chin and sighed at all the right places. But when I got to the part about him letting me go, he said, "Can't let you go, son. Oh, I understand you got dealt a bad hand. But there's not much I can do. Can't just let you go, not after the County's gone to the trouble of arresting and sentencing you. They'd say I aided your flight and escape, say I'd abetted the delinquency of a minor. It would land me in a mess of hot water. And I got the Lord's work to do," he said, making me sag with heartache. "I'll tell you what I'll do. I'll talk to the County people and make 'em understand the injustice of it. How's that?"

He had held out his hand, and said, "I promise."

I figured it was a square deal and the best one I was gonna get, so I shook.

"I want to help you boys any way I can. Been down-and-out myself. More'n once! It's the Lord's work to help boys like you!" he bellowed with a voice that rolled out of him like the chime from a big bell.

Later, me and the colored kid found the last spare space on the floor to sleep. I didn't like being tucked in so close to him, but there wasn't anywhere else to go, so I just closed my eyes and dreamed about catching up with Little Bill.

"**C**ome on, mutts. Gotta get the trash out," Pig Ears said, awakening us with the toe of his shoe.

We tiptoed through the predawn darkness and around the sleeping homeless. I rubbed my eyes and stumbled over the colored kid, who seemed to have come fully awake in a blink.

We went to the kitchen, where several large garbage cans

spilled potato and carrot peelings. We got on the opposite sides of one and lifted.

"What the heck are you doing?" Pig Ears asked, unlocking the back door.

"Throwing out the garbage," I said.

"Geez, not that trash. *That trash,*" he said, tilting his head back toward the room full of people. "But before we roust them, we gotta feed 'em. We gotta run over to the bakery and pick up hard rolls," he said.

After a short drive, me and the colored kid found ourselves loading bags of rolls. As we tossed in the last of them, Pig Ears left us to pay the baker.

The colored kid watched until he disappeared, and said, "Let's bolt."

"No!" I cried. A botched escape would ruin any chance of Papa Bear helping me. The thought of having to stay the full month or maybe even longer scared the heck out of me. I grabbed the kid's arm. "You're gonna mess everything up!"

"Let go, ya little creep!" he grunted as he tried to shake himself free.

Pig Ears returned. Seeing us struggle, he said, "Stop your horsing around!"

Back at the mission, we brought the rolls into the kitchen, where a volunteer brewed coffee in giant pots. Papa Bear strolled in, clapped his hands, and said, "Great work!" Pig Ears banged a pot lid with a spoon, waking the crowd. They filed into the kitchen, where we handed out rolls and coffee.

The colored kid growled, "I'll get you."

Papa Bear blessed everyone, and Pig Ears shooed them out the door. We were ordered to sweep and mop the basement floor. I tried to ignore the hard glances the kid shot me as I pushed the broom around.

Pig Ears pointed to buckets, and we filled them in the kitchen. Overflowing with water, they were heavy. I could barely lift mine. The other kid spilled soapy water over my foot. He grinned. It wasn't an accident.

Mopping is kinda like dancing with a clumsy, skinny clown with big feet. I didn't like it. Pig Ears walked through the basement. As he passed, one foot slipped, sending him sailing and spreading his legs wide.

"Holy Jeez!" he cried, somehow pulling himself up.

We could barely keep a straight face, but it was the colored kid who got it from Pig Ears.

"Stupid darkie! Can't even mop? Leave puddles for people to slip on? Never met one of you who could do even half a job right!" he shouted. "If it was up to me, you would have gone to the County Lockup first thing, or out on a chain gang with the rest of the darkies!"

As he chewed out the kid, I quietly moved my bucket behind him.

"You just better follow the straight-and-narrow from now on. You understand, or are you a simpleton?" he yelled.

"I understand," the kid said through clenched teeth.

Pig Ears spun around to leave, took a step, and dropped his foot into my bucket.

"What the . . . !" he cried.

I was far away, mopping the opposite corner of the

basement. He cursed and stomped away. After he'd gone, the kid caught my eye and nodded.

That night found us pressed together again.

"What's your name?" he asked.

"Collie," I said.

"Ike," he said, adding, "Ya know, Papa Bear ain't gonna lift a finger for you."

"I think he's being square with us. Promised to help. Promised to get me outa here lickety-split," I said.

"Don't be a blockhead!"

"I ain't a blockhead."

"You're right, you're not a blockhead. You're a sap. That bunk the Big Bear fed you. Assisting escape. Abetting delinquency. You swallowed it hook, line, and sinker. Think about this: how much does he pay you to peel potatoes, haul tables, and such?"

"Nothing."

"Yeah, nothin'! So, do you think he wants you around 'cause he's afraid of what the County would do if you ran off, or because he don't want to lose a work-for-nothing sap like you?"

"Aww, you're full of hooey," I said.

"Believe what you want. You pulled a swell fast one when that nose-picker soaked his foot. I just wanted to pay you back," he said, curling himself into his blanket.

He fell asleep right away. I laid there for a long time. Thinking.

Mornings were the same. We'd wake and feed the crowd. Afterward, me and Ike got to eat—coffee and hard rolls. Lunch was hit-or-miss, depending on who the volunteer cook was, then soup and hard rolls for dinner.

Little Man Burp—that's what I called him because he belched all the time—rapped our hands with a wooden spoon if we reached for a carrot or bit of celery.

"Mitts off!" he'd squeak.

"You'd think he'd paid for this stuff," Ike muttered.

Mrs. Rote was nicer. She'd make a baloney or ham sandwich and serve it up to us on a plate and with a napkin, like we were customers in a regular restaurant. It steamed Pig Ears to see her treat us so fine, but he kept his yap shut. She had known Papa Bear before Pig Ears and, according to Papa Bear, could do no wrong.

I'd like to say Pig Ears, creep that he was, had it better than us, but he didn't. I didn't see anything go into his belly that didn't go into ours.

Papa Bear was different. His appetite matched his size, big, and he wolfed down huge meals: bacon and eggs for breakfast, and pork or beef or roast chicken for dinner. I never saw Little Man Burp or Mrs. Rote fix supper for him. It was delivered, mostly by cops.

Go figure.

Soup dinners were okay at first, but me and Ike tired of them pretty quick.

"Not as good as a mulligan stew," Ike said.

"And a lot thinner," I added.

Our stomachs growled all the time, and we were always
on the lookout to swipe carrots and potatoes, dredging them
out of the cook pots.

One day, Papa Bear arrived with a load of chickens and
told Mrs. Rote to make soup.

"There's not enough birds to feed everyone on the soup
line," she said.

"Sure there is. This is what you do: Let 'em stew for just
a little while. Then move 'em into another pot, and let 'em
stew there, too. Then another. This way, we can spread the
flavor around, you see. Add carrots, potatoes, and such,
divvy the chicken meat among the pots, a little here, a little
there, and you should be able to get six pots out of 'em.
Maybe eight. That should do it, shouldn't it, Mrs. Rote?"

He started out of the kitchen, turning back to her to say,
"But save one of the birds for me, okay?"

Mrs. Rote smiled and nodded.

She set us to cleaning vegetables and shuffling the birds
from pot to pot like musical chairs. Fishing the hot birds
out of the soup with big spoons wasn't an easy trick without cooking your fingers, too, but we were keen for the job
anyways.

Bits of cooked bird fell off the bones at each swap and
we snatched up the pieces, blew on them for a second, and
then popped them into our mouths. It was the best meal we
had at the mission and made up for the hard work.

"Papa Bear would say we were stealing," I said.

"He'd have to say it with a mouth full of chicken, himself," Ike replied.

Days passed and we made soup, cleaned pots, carried blankets, and moved tables. We cleaned potatoes one day. Papa Bear walked past and gave me the high sign, quick to add he'd be talking to the County right off. Ike snorted quietly.

"He's gonna come through," I said to Ike.

"He talking through his hat, you dope," he replied.

We skinned potato after potato.

"This is the crummiest job ever," I muttered.

"Then you never picked cotton," Ike said, cleaning a big potato and plunking it into a pot. "What is that, the millionth I've done to your *one*?"

Ike worked a lot faster than me, peeling the potatoes one-two-three, while I slowly hacked away, gouging chunks off until all that was left was hardly bigger than a marble. But fast or slow, it was boring, and me and Ike sighed.

"So, is all that stuff you said about searching for your brother on the up-and-up, or was it just a line you were running?" Ike asked.

"Ain't no line," I said.

"Seems to me that brother of yours should have had the good sense to stick around and help you and your ma," he said.

"You only heard a part of it. It's a long story," I said.

"Yeah, and we're going somewhere?" he asked, tilting his head to the mountain of potatoes to be cleaned.

I told him the whole thing, including the stuff I'd hid from Papa Bear: Little Bill's drinking and him smacking me around.

"I still don't understand why you're chasing all over God's creation after him," Ike said, removing a thin slice of skin from a potato.

"You got a big family?" I asked.

"Sure do. Ten of us. Seven brothers and two sisters. And a mess of cousins, too many to count," he said.

"All we got is us. Then we lost my dad. Now my brother's gone," I said, lifting a potato I'd started cleaning. "It's like this potato. You keep hacking pieces away and pretty soon there's nothing left."

Pig Ears interrupted us and ordered me to mop the chapel floor. I gathered a bucket and mop and met Ike as he cleaned the large storefront window. Papa Bear and Pig Ears walked to the front door, talking excitedly about a "big show."

The men climbed into a black sedan and drove off.

Me and the Ike kid worked in silence. Bright sunlight flooded the room. The temperature climbed and sweat dribbled down my armpits. I opened the front door, hoping to catch a slight breeze. When I turned back to my mop, I met Ike's wide eyes.

"Whatsamatter?" I asked.

"I swear I'm getting as dopey as you," he said.

"What are you talking about?"

"The door. It's unlocked."

"So what?"

"So what! So, we can get out of here. Beat it. Hit the bricks!"

"They'll catch us and throw us into the County Lockup," I said.

"We beat it to the rails and hop a freight," Ike said.

"No. Papa Bear said he'd get me sprung, and I'm throwing in with him," I said.

"Forget him! He's a flimflam man. Come on, let's go before it's too late. They could come back any time."

"No. You go."

"Don't be a sap. This is your golden chance!"

"What's it to you?"

"Heading out alone to fetch your brother, for your ma. It ain't easy. I know. Don't want ya getting the short end of the stick."

The black car returned. We quickly started cleaning again. Papa Bear and Pig Ears strolled in. Papa Bear gave us a thumbs-up, saying, "Swell work!"

Pig Ears noticed the open door, and locked it.

After they'd gone, I said, "Sorry, Ike. That's the second time I've messed up your chances."

He shook his head, and looked low.

Later in the kitchen, Papa Bear announced the big news.

"A Campground Meeting!" Papa Bear explained to everyone. Out in the countryside, under a tent, he said.

"You'll be working like devils to get ready," he promised, and he was right. We worked around the clock, right up to that morning a week later when we loaded four trucks and struck out for the site.

We sped over a rough country road, passing parched fields and stirring up clouds of dust that left a dirty film all over us and the load of chairs we were squeezed beside.

"Not today, Collie," Papa Bear had said when I asked him if he'd talked to County about springing me early. "Keep your mind on loading those chairs."

Ike overheard and said, "You got too many eggs in the Papa Bear basket."

Ike never missed a chance to tell me I was a dope for trusting Papa Bear. Other than that, him and me got along, which was good because we had only each other. The other Mission people were grown, and barely gave us the time of day beyond orders to peel, scrub, and carry. So me and Ike peeled potatoes together, scrubbed floors together, washed dishes together. We ate together and slept in the same tiny corner of the room together. I told him my story and he told me his.

Ike was a sharecropper's son and had been on the road for a couple of years.

"Your pa threw you out when you were just twelve?" I asked.

"Didn't throw me out! I had to leave. There were too many mouths and too little food. I was the oldest. My place to leave," he explained.

He'd been almost everywhere.

"Seen the Atlantic and the Pacific Oceans," he boasted. "I've shined shoes, canned fish, and picked berries. I've eaten *chop suey*!"

Said he could spot a sharpie from a mile off, and that Papa Bear was one.

"A pastor?" I asked.

"Sure. Sharpies come in all flavors. Men. Women. White folks. Colored. Rich. Poor. There are God-fearing sharpies and God-forgetting sharpies."

"I dunno. Haven't we seen Papa Bear get alkies off the booze, pull bums from the gutter, and feed a mess of people for free?"

"Maybe so, but I still don't trust him."

Papa Bear rode in a sedan leading the trucks. After an hour's drive, we pulled off the road and onto a large field. It was busy-as-beavers' time then. The tent got raised, a platform built, and chairs unloaded. A makeshift kitchen went up so we could sell food.

"Place them chairs in rows. They should all be pointing at the stage in the center where I'll be speaking," Papa Bear said as Ike and me unloaded the chairs.

It was stifling beneath the tent, and the hot, trapped air puffed out the canvas like a balloon.

"Ever been to a campground revival meeting?" I asked.

"When I was a kid," Ike said. "My pa didn't like the

preacher saying everyone was going to hell, even little babies. Pa didn't believe a baby could sin bad enough to go to hell. So we never went again."

We placed the last chairs, and Pig Ears arrived with a pitcher of lemonade, saying, "The pastor sent this for you. Made a point that you two get taken care of."

"See, I told you he's all right," I said to Ike, gulping the lemonade.

Weeeee-000000000.

A train's whistle. Far off, but a train's whistle, all the same.

We raced outside.

"Off that way?" I asked.

"Can't tell. The sound is bouncing around like a ball off a wall," he said. "Spy any smoke?"

"Nothing," I said, after looking all around for the telltale signs of a locomotive.

"Means the rails ain't nearby," he said.

WEEEE-0000000.

"Aw, who cares anyway? It's not like we're gonna jump a train or anything," I said.

"It's not?" Ike asked.

Papa Bear appeared and said, "Better grab some food, boys. Won't have the chance later. Collie, the sheriff promised he'd visit. I'm hopin' I'll have the chance to mention you."

"See," I said to Ike as we headed to the makeshift kitchen. Ike just shook his head. At the kitchen, we got cheese sandwiches and lemonade, and didn't talk anymore about the train.

People arrived just past dusk: Farmers in white shirts and stained overalls, women in plain dresses pressed as flat as the thin, worn fabric would take an iron, kids in hand-me-downs, most without shoes. They fanned themselves with hats and hands.

Papa Bear made his way to the center platform, glad-handing people as he walked, smiling and nodding, too. Stepping to the middle of the platform, he raised his arms, and the chattering and squirming ended.

"It's tough times. Tough times! The Good Lord knows it. He knows it's tough times, and he wants to help!" he boomed like thunder. Then he let rip a fire-and-brimstone sermon, about injustice and mercy and temptation and the ways of Satan. "There's a path," he told them.

"Take the right path. It's out there, children! The right path is waiting for you. Just take the first step! Salvation awaits!" he cried, his arm outstretched to the sky.

People, alone, in couples, in groups, rose from their chairs. They wept with joy, threw themselves at Papa Bear's feet, and begged to be shown the way. Papa Bear lifted them up, wrapped his enormous arms around them, hugged them, and wept with them.

I was spellbound. Elbowing Ike, I asked, "You still think he's a sharpie?"

After Papa Bear finished saving souls, the audience streamed out of the steaming tent, desperate for a drink. We sold them gallons of lemonade. The pennies and nickels they handed over for it collected in buckets at Papa Bear's feet.

"Great sermon!" "Wonderful sermon!" "Thank you!" "Bless you!" People called to him, and he just waved off the praise and blushed.

It was midnight before everyone left and we could clean up. Ike and me scrubbed pots as Papa Bear and Pig Ears talked nearby.

"Could have made more if we'd had more lemonade," Papa Bear said, staring into the money buckets. "Make sure we don't make the same mistake tomorrow."

Pig Ears nodded.

"Do you think we drew a bigger crowd than the Salvation Army would have?" Papa Bear asked.

"Sure we did. Tomorrow will be even bigger. You're doing great, boss," Pig Ears said as the two men left.

Everything went back into the trucks, and we headed back to the Spearmint Street Mission. The rough ride didn't stop me dozing the whole trip. I sleepwalked inside, not suspecting that this would be my last night sleeping on the Mission's basement floor.

Papa Bear woke us early. We loaded trucks and drove back to the Revival field. The tent went up, and me and Ike filled it with chairs again. Then Papa Bear took us to the kitchen, where we found a mountain of lemons.

"Don't want anyone to leave thirsty," Papa Bear said, telling us to squeeze each and every one of them. As he left, he added, "Collie, the county sheriff is definitely coming. I'm gonna tell him all about your problem."

It was swell news! I could almost ignore the lemon juice stinging the million little cuts I had on my hands from moving the chairs.

Ike asked, "Do you think we'll hear another train today?"

"Geez, Ike, I don't care. Papa Bear said he's gonna talk with the sheriff. I'm banking on that, not some harebrained scheme of running off and finding a freight."

We squeezed an ocean of juice until all that was left was a giant pile of squashed lemons. Pig Ears told us to dump them in the trees behind the kitchen. We picked up buckets and trudged across the dirty field and into the woods. Pushing deep into the brush, we reached a sunny clearing, about the size of a schoolyard. I threw down the lemons and started hiking back to the kitchen.

Thwack!

A lemon splattered against my shoulder. Bits of it sprayed the side of my face.

Thwack!

Another sailed past me and hit a tree.

"Hey!" I shouted.

Ike laughed and winged another lemon at me.

I grabbed one, and the war was on. We darted back and forth across the clearing, tossing lemons. Ike let loose a barrage of lemons that hit me in the shoulder, stomach, and thigh.

"Ya got me!" I blurted, falling down dead like the villains in the picture shows.

Ike dropped to the ground, too, and we belly-laughed.

I spied a broken tree branch on the ground, snatched it up, and swung it like a Louisville Slugger, and said, "Pitch one in!"

Ike took a lemon and backed away to a good pitching distance. "I'll give you my best Satchel Paige triple windup!" he shouted, jiggling his knee and spinning his arm like a windmill.

He threw a straight, waist-high lemon-ball, and I smacked it square, exploding both the lemon and the bat into smithereens.

"We need a better bat!" I said, and the two of us searched the clearing. "Find anything?" I called to Ike yards away.

He lifted his hands for silence.

"What's up?" I asked.

He raised his hand again, adding a nasty glare to boot. Then he dropped to one knee. I fell to the ground and crawled to him.

"Somebody's out there," he whispered.

Creeping forward, we came to the tree line and the road leading to the Revival field. Two cars were parked on its shoulder, and a couple of guys were standing behind them. One was Papa Bear.

"Great crowd last night! Hope to do better tonight," he bellowed.

"Sure you will. Pretty soon, you'll have the biggest Mission in town. Make the Salvation Army look like a flea circus in comparison," the other man said.

"Thanks, Sheriff," Papa Bear said.

The Sheriff!

"It's the truth," said the Sheriff. "And I'm counting on it. Got ya some more hands. Three new transfers for you. And not like the two guppies you took last time. Big ones. Sure you'll find work for them."

"Yes, I will."

"Oh, I almost forgot. Here's the money for those two transfers."

The Sheriff handed Papa Bear a wad of cash.

The Sheriff said, "Paying you to take them hooligans is cheaper than jailin' 'em ourselves."

"Speaking of them two. I've got another Revival meeting—a big one—planned for three weeks from now, and I can use all the help I can get. You think you could convince the judge to extend their sentence until I'm done with them?"

"Shouldn't be a problem. The judge knows the good work you do, and the boys are probably better off with you anyway."

"You're a lifesaver, Sheriff. And I never forget my friends," Papa Bear said, handing the Sheriff five bills peeled from the wad of money.

The men shook hands and left, leaving dust tails from their speeding cars.

Extend their service!

The words hit me like punches. My head fell over like my neck muscles were snipped.

"I told you he was a sharpie who just wants to make some dough off us and build up his lousy Mission. The miserable, lying creep!" Ike barked.

We stared into the dirt.

"You still think there's a train somewhere out there?" I finally asked.

He nodded.

"Well, let's find it, because I'm not going back," I said.

"You bet!" Ike said.

"I'm all turned around. Which way did we think the rails were?" I asked.

Looking around and pointing, Ike said, "The tent's back there. I say the tracks are that-a-way."

We headed off in the direction of his pointed finger, walking at first and then, without saying a word, running.

"**C**ome on!" Ike yelled as we raced through the woods. He flew ahead, while weeds and low branches grabbed my ankles and slowed me down. Then we burst from the trees, and a huge open field, flat and brown, unrolled in front of us, separating us from the next stand of trees.

"We gotta keep going. But out there, in the open, we're gonna stick out," I said.

"Like a bonnet on a mule," Ike said.

"We gotta get past this open field as fast as we can. Once

we start, we can't stop. So get your breath. It's gonna be a long, long run," I said.

We sucked air into our lungs until we got lightheaded and then darted off. The sun was bright and hot. Ike ran ahead and kicked dust into me. Sweat tickled my neck and sides. I huffed like a locomotive. We ran and ran, but the distant trees didn't seem to get any closer. It was crazy.

"Gotta stop," I gasped.

"Don't!" Ike grunted, grabbing my arm and pulling me.

Sweat ran into my eyes and everything looked screwy, like in a funhouse mirror.

"Almost there," Ike said.

Finally, we plunged into the woods, and I collapsed into the cool shade. I swallowed large slices of air, and waited for my heart to stop pounding.

"How long do you think we've been gone?" Ike asked.

"More than an hour, I guess," I said.

"I don't think they'll come after us. I think they got more important things to do than chase kids like us," Ike said.

I shrugged. I wasn't going to let them take me back.

Weee-ooo.

"It's near!" Ike said.

Weee-ooOO.

The whistle led us through the wood, and tall brush, until we came to a wide stream beside a beautiful set of railroad tracks. I had one foot in the stream when Ike mumbled, "I can't swim."

Weee-OOOO.

I saw a locomotive's smoke rise down the tracks.

"Then we gotta find something you can float across on," I said. Spotting a dead tree with arms of big, long branches, I shouted, "There! We can break off a big one!"

We leaped for the lowest one, but it was just beyond our reach.

"Lift me!" I cried.

Ike slipped beneath me and raised me on his shoulders. I grabbed the end of the branch but couldn't break it free.

"Stay there!" Ike shouted, leaving me dangling. He leaped up and latched onto my shoulders. We bounced up and down together until the branch snapped and we crashed to the ground like a pheasant shot out of the sky.

Dragging that branch to the stream was murder. It was heavy and had small branches that plowed the ground and stabbed other trees. Finally, we got it to the water and threw it in. I hopped in after it.

Ike stood on the bank as still as a statue.

I remembered what it was like not knowing how to swim and having scary thoughts of drowning. I said, "Ike, I'll get you across."

We plunged into the water, and hugged the branch. I pushed us forward.

"Kick!" I shouted.

Ike thrashed with his feet while I did the same, all the while clawing the water with a free hand. I was sure we were gonna make it when suddenly, in midstream, Ike slipped off, made a panic grab for me, and tore me free of the branch, too. We sank. Water choked me. I flung my hand out, caught the branch, and pulled us up. Gasping, we got a sure grip and started paddling again. Finally, I dragged the branch and Ike ashore. We looked up and saw the locomotive and long tail of boxcars rumbling past.

WEEE-OOOOO!!!

We scrambled after it. I grabbed a handrail and swung into an open boxcar. Ike followed, but slipped, and fell half out. I yanked him in by his shirt.

Dripping wet and panting heavy, I looked outside for the Revival tent in the distance, but saw only scrubby fields.

"Wonder where we're going," Ike said.

I remembered what Scarecrow had said when I'd asked the same question: "Somewhere else."

The miles between us and Papa Bear grew, and Ike and me breathed easier. But the southbound freight was taking me farther and farther from Little Bill. We'd have to jump another train soon.

"We gotta find a jungle and a hobo who can tell us how to go west," I said.

At dusk, the freight slowed, and approached a rail yard. Me and Ike hopped off. We trudged down a narrow lane in search of a jungle or a town, but we found only more road. Darkness was falling, I started to look around at the brush for a good place to sleep when Ike spotted a large, flat-roofed shack of bare wood and rusty metal.

It leaned like a house of cards. A dented chimney pipe

stuck up from its roof, leaking gray-white smoke. Rickety steps led to a crooked landing, where a crude door hung. Nailed beside the door were faded metal signs for Jax Beer and Chero Cola. Hand-painted above the door was *Sooter's*.

"A barrelhouse," Ike said.

I shrugged.

"A juke joint," he tried.

"Juke joint?"

Ike sighed and said, "Just wait here while I get the skinny."

He went inside, brushing past two colored men coming out, each carrying a chair and a beer bottle. They plopped themselves down and drank, giving me odd looks. I made designs in the dirt with the tip of my shoe.

Ike returned and said, "We can sleep in the barn in the back, Ain't much of a place, walls's missing slats and there's holes in the roof. But there's clean hay, so we won't have to stretch out on the ground. Get a meal, too. All we got to do is split some firewood."

"That's swell!" I said.

"Here's the thing. This is a colored place. Ain't gonna be no white folk except you," he said.

"I don't got no problem with that."

"Well, that don't mean they don't."

"They don't want me to be here?"

Ike said, "White folks got their joints and colored folks theirs. But I convinced 'em. Told 'em you were soft in the head. Told 'em I was looking out for you."

"Geez, soft in the head. How am I supposed to act?"

"Act yourself," Ike said.

He led me to the back of the shack, where a whole pig roasted on a spit over an open fire. A shirtless man slowly turned the spit. The pig sizzled, and the man's skin shined with sweat. A pile of wood stood nearby.

The shirtless man eyed me and said to Ike, "Y'all make sure that idiot doesn't chop off his own foot, ya hear?"

"Yes, sir," Ike replied, shooting me a sly grin.

We split wood in the light of the fire. Ike took first licks, swinging hard and splitting most pieces with one strike. Me, I wasn't as good. I thought I was chopping down strong, but more times than not, the ax head just got stuck in the wood. Then I'd have to swing them together, and try to bring the pair down hard enough to split the wood.

It was my first clumsy try with an ax. Little Bill had used Dad's old ax to chop wood for our fireplace.

"Didn't you tell me your dad was a lumberjack?" Ike snickered with a laugh.

"Aww, shut up!" I said.

It took me twice as long as Ike to split the same number of logs. I got as shiny with sweat as the pig-cooker man and was glad when we got to the bottom of the woodpile. We went inside and sat. Sooter, the pig-cook, handed us plates of shredded pork swimming in a ketchup-and-molasses sauce. We went at it like dogs.

Colored men trudged and filled the juke joint. "Turpentine men," Ike said, explaining he'd heard there was a place in the pines making the stuff. The men stunk of it, and only clouds of cigarette smoke disguised the biting smell. Women joined the men. Everybody drank beer and gobbled pork. They joked, laughed, and cursed. The room heated up, sweat stained everyone's clothes. Calls for more cold beer came more often and louder.

My white face got more than a few surprised looks, making me feel like the uninvited guest at a party.

"Wanna head to the barn?" I asked Ike.

"Hang on, Collie. Let's wait for the music," he said.

"Music?" I asked, but my question drowned in the clapping and shouts for an old colored man making his way to a stool in the corner of the room. He looked like a tortoise. Waving off the applause, he picked up a scuffed guitar. His bald head started swaying to a silent beat, and his bulging turtle eyes closed. He started plucking notes from his battered guitar, crazy notes that cried like a train whistle and sobbed like a baby. The crowd hushed except for a few murmurs of "Sing it, brother," the same way someone might call out "amen" in church.

That old tortoise sang about losing money, losing friends, losing your home, and losing your love. Sad things, things that would make you cry.

He sang,

> Oh Lord, I'm so low down.
> Oh, Lord, I'm so low down.
> My misery's a storm,
> Blowin' me from town to town.

Me and Ike listened until we were punchy from tiredness. We went to the barn and curled up in the fresh hay. Tortoise's voice carried right through, and I fell asleep to it.

Ike and me meant to hightail it out of there the first thing after waking, but Sooter had more wood to chop and another four bits for doing it. We decided fifty cents in our pockets was more important than an early start, and spent the best part of the morning swinging axes. When we finished, Ike went to collect the dough. I fell down beside the woodpile and rubbed the blisters on my hands.

I was still on the ground when he raced back, crying, "Just heard Sooter talking to a guy buying a Chero Cola. Said he was heading to the next town. We could hop a freight there!"

We sprinted to the front of the juke joint and spotted a colored guy ambling toward a beat-up sedan, soda pop in hand.

"Hey!" I cried.

The whole story gushed out of us, how we were stranded and needed to jump a train in the next town and wouldn't it be great if we could shag a ride—

"Take a breath!" the large man said.

"Yes, sir! We wouldn't be no trouble and hardly take up any room since it's just us and no stuff. And we got a buck to kick for expenses, too," I said.

"Dunno, kid," the large man said as he slipped into the car. "Not really interested in carrying passengers, paying or not."

"We could help out. Carry your stuff," I said, spying

trunks and suitcases lashed to the running boards of the car.

"Don't need another pair of hands to do what I do alone now," he said, yawning and rubbing his puffy, blood-shot eyes.

The guy was beat, exhausted!

"I could drive you! Be your, uh, chauffeur," I said.

"What the heck are you talking about? Drive? You're just a kid, kid. You pulling my leg?" he asked.

"No sir! I know how to drive. Swear I can drive! Work the clutch and the gears and everything. Swear I'm not pulling your leg," I said.

The man drummed the steering wheel.

"And when I'm driving, you can nap," I said.

Moments dragged as the large driver rubbed his eyes and thought.

"He can do it, mister. I seen him with my own eyes," Ike lied.

Finally, the man said, "I'm not jumping into the backseat until I've seen you drive. Show me your stuff, kid."

I got behind the wheel. The driver slid over, and Ike got into the back. My foot shivered as it pushed down the clutch, and I slipped the car into first gear.

"Come on, kid," the man said. "Don't want to grow old here."

I took a deep breath and let the clutch up without stalling. Throwing the gears right up to third, we left the juke joint behind and found the road, high-balling along at thirty miles an hour. I think it was thirty, because my eyes were glued to the road, me being too afraid to look down at the speedometer.

"I knew you could do it. I knew it!" Ike yelled from the backseat, slapping my shoulder and jarring my steering hands. In a blink we were off the road and flying into a cornfield.

We plunged into the corn, bounced over a drainage ditch on the way, smashing our heads against the car ceiling. I barely held onto the steering wheel. Cornstalks slapped the car as we rattled over furrows. I turned sharply, tilting us on two wheels. We bounced over the drainage ditch again, and shot back onto the road like a squirted watermelon seed. After a few crazy back-and-forths, I straightened us out and got us rolling along like nothing had happened.

The large man was pressed against the door, and Ike lay stretched out over the backseat, the two of them gripping the seat cushions like they were lifebouys.

"Did I pass the test?" I asked.

The man exploded in laughter. When he was down to snorts, he said, "Stop the car."

I guessed this was where we'd get the bum's rush. But then the large man climbed into the backseat, forcing Ike to move into the front.

"Drive, kid," he said, sliding down and closing his eyes.

"Really?" I asked.

He nodded.

"Sure thing!" I chirped. Working the clutch, the gas, and the gears as slick as could be, I got us going again. Behind me, the guy muttered, *"Did I pass the test?"*

We drove west through baked-brown farmland under a cloudless blue sky. Nothing changed except the height of the bright sun and the direction of the sharp shadows it threw. A weather-beaten shack selling gas and food appeared beside the road. We filled up on fuel, and I bought some chewing gum.

Back on the road, we passed fields covered in the stubble, like a hobo's three-day beard. Barbed wire held up by bony wood posts ran along the road.

A crossroads arrived. *Straight, right, left?*

"I'm stumped," the guy in the backseat said.

"You ain't never been here before?" Ike asked.

"Sorry, kid. This is my first pass," he said.

I sighed. The endless drive now offered a chance of getting lost.

Ike said, "I say straight."

"Geez, how would you know? You never been here," I protested. "I say we turn."

"You neither," he replied.

I blinked sweat from my eyes.

"Turn," I said.

"Straight," Ike replied.

"Turn."

"Holy cow, you're stubborn. A blacksmith could use your head for an anvil."

"Hey, Mister, do you know the difference between Ike here and a dumbbell?"

"No," he said.

"See Ike, he can't tell the difference, either!" I said.

The man exploded with laughter. He wiped his eye, and sank into his seat. "Ezra Jobe. Now there was the dumbest man I ever knew.

"Ol' Ezra sharecropped for the Seese family. In fact the Jobes and the Seeses went way back, what with Captain Seese owning Ezra's granddaddy for a spell. Anyway, Ezra wasn't bright. In fact, you could say the mules pulling his smarts had up and died. Out of the blue, Ezra decided he should go to school, even though he's all grown and never been before. He trudged to the schoolhouse and asks to enroll.

"Do you know your ABC's?" the little old schoolmarm asked him.

"Ol' Ezra thinks and thinks and thinks. Finally, he says, 'I know Debbie Seese and I know Robbie Seese, but I don't know any *Abie Seese!*'"

Ike and me laughed like a couple of donkeys.

Together, we decided to take the left turn.

Hours later, we reached a town. The man directed me down a street to a theater. The marquee read *Ray "Rainy" Knight Performing Tonite!*

"Who the heck is 'Rainy' Knight?" I asked.

"Me, kid," came a voice from the backseat.

"You're an actor, or something?" I asked.

"Yeah, something. A comic," Rainy said, getting out of the car. He stared up at the marquee. "At least they spelled my name right."

"But this place is a movie house," Ike said.

"The place piggybacks live acts with the motion picture show," he explained. "Okay, one of you help me bring the stuff in. The other can watch the car."

Ike grabbed for the suitcases and followed Rainy into the theater. I rested against the car. The bright white sun heated the Dodge, and the fender began cooking my backside. I pushed away from the car and stood in the shade of the marquee.

Two boys wandered up to the Dodge. They were about my age. One carried a shoeshine kit, and the other chewed gum. Their white shirts were dingy but still stood out against their black skins.

"A straight six or a V-eight?" asked the gum chewer.

"Not sure," replied the shoe shiner, who found his reflection in the windshield and preened at the image.

The first boy circled the car and poked his head through the open driver's side window.

I didn't like that.

"Hey!" I called, trying to make my voice hard the way the bulls did when they warned you away from the rails.

Both boys turned, but slowly, like they hadn't a care in the world. They eyed me for a moment, then the shoe shiner asked, "You with this car?"

"Yeah. I'm the driver," I said, puffing up my chest.

The boy rolled his eyes, saying, "The driver? You don't look old enough to be no driver. I bet you're nothing but a lookout. Bet somebody paid you a nickel to watch out for his car, thaz all."

"I'm the driver, I'm telling ya. Keep away from the car, okay?" I said.

"Keep away from it? You hear that? Said we should keep away from it," the boy said to his friend. They both laughed, and the shoeshine boy dropped his kit. They got close, moving apart so that one stopped directly in front of me and the other was split to the side. Trying to keep both in view, I stepped back. They stepped with me.

Shoeshine pushed his face into mine and asked, "Straight six or V-eight?"

"Dunno," I said.

"How can ya be the driver and not know the engine? Doesn't seem square. Maybe you're just a fat-mouthed wise guy trying to pull a fast one on a couple of country boys," he said, shoving me hard.

"Whadaya think you're doing?" Ike called from the theater door. He came to my side and faced the boys. "No call for you to fuss with my pal."

"Your pal? Why would you pal with *him*?" Shoeshine sneered.

"Don't have to answer your questions. And if there are questions then I'm gonna be the one asking 'em, like how you got to be such a low-down-dumb-as-a-monkey fool?" Ike laughed.

Shoeshine's fist crashed into Ike's head, sending him stumbling backwards.

"My hand!" Shoeshine started crying, holding his limp right hand with the left. It was swollen and purple. He blew on it, shook it. It seemed Ike's forehead was harder than the kid's fist.

Ike had Shoeshine against the car. He socked him in the stomach, and the kid slid to his knees with a moan. His pal ran off.

I snatched up his shoeshine kit and flung it to the ground, cracking the box's seams. Leaping onto it, I shattered the wood and scattered the tins of shoe polish and brushes.

"Yeah, how do you like that?" Ike yelled, kicking the pieces into the gutter.

The kid cradled his broken hand and staggered away. Ike held his head.

"Lemme see," I said. "Nothing. Not bleeding. Just a little lump."

As he rubbed his hurt noggin, I asked. "What about the comic guy?"

"Told us to park the jalopy in the back. Said we could watch his show for free. Said he could get you a ticket for a regular seat if you wanted it, no problem, but I gotta stay hidden in the back. It's a 'whites only' theater."

"Nah. I'll watch with you," I said.

Me and Ike waited for the theater to go dark before we snuck in and pressed ourselves against the back wall. Ike kept his cap pulled low to hide. But the audience was excited about seeing the motion picture and never even glanced back at us.

The show didn't start right away. The crowd gabbed, kids joked, babies cried, and the heat rose.

"We're slow cooking," I complained, feeling sweat dribble down my back.

People started clapping in unison, and then chanted, "We want the show! We want the show!"

The only thing they got was hotter and louder.

"Come on! Let's get going!" someone shouted.

An apple core flew at the blank screen and then an empty cigarette pack.

Sweat trailed down my back, and I complained, " Geez, who's in charge?"

"What's your hurry? We got a big dinner waiting for us at home?" Ike asked.

Finally, the projector started clicking and everyone hushed up, as quiet as church mice. Crazy blurred images splashed across the screen while the projectionist focused, and then the movie finally started. Actually, it was a bunch of movies, silents all, which kinda disappointed me, the talkies being a lot better. Still, there was the Keystone Kops, and you can't lose with them. Then there was a funny two-reeler that ends with Ben Turpin getting a pie in the kisser, which I missed because the lug in front of me stood up to swat some kid sassing his girlfriend.

Harold Lloyd, Fatty Arbuckle, Buster Keaton, and Charlie Chaplin flickered by, and a few *Perils of Pauline*, too. An hour passed before the projector went off.

The theater stunk of sweat, mildew, and cigarette smoke. People began to rise from their seats and head for the exits.

I was about to ask Ike where Rainy was, when he shuffled on stage.

"Y'all leaving gonna miss the tip-toppist comic wowin' 'tainment circles from Broadway to Knob Hill," he drawled. "I is that, the funniest darkie y'all ever come across in the whole $U \ldots S \ldots of \ldots A \ldots$ and if you leave now, y'all gonna miss the show."

His voice was entirely different from the one we'd known from our ride. He wore baggy pants, cream-colored, high-waisted things that came all the way up to his chest, and cut so large that I bet they woulda fallen down if it wasn't for his red suspenders. A straw boater a size too small topped his head. But his clothes, oddball as they were, weren't the craziest thing about his looks.

Though he was plainly a colored man, he'd blackened his face and painted his lips white, and he looked like something you might see in a minstrel show poster.

"What's on his face?" I asked.

"Burnt cork," Ike replied.

"Why's that?" I asked.

"You people don't want to see colored folks, you want to see someone playing colored folks," he said.

You people? I never thought of myself as "you people."

Rainy cracked jokes, some good, some awful, but at such a clip that the laughs from the good jokes spilled over onto the bad ones until everything seemed funny, and the crowd laughed non-stop. A mug near us hee-hawed at the gags, slapping his girlfriend on the back at every punch line, while she winced at every slap. I was all teeth and grins, and so was Ike.

Rainy switched from jokes to stories, all of them about how dumb he was. He they talked about the Depression, or the "'Pression."

"Dis here 'Pression making me powerful angry at white folks," he announced. "Before, the only thing black folks could call their own was poverty, and now white folks have up and taken dat too!"

He finished with a few songs, hacking away at the melodies.

At the end he got thumping applause and cheering. If it had been election day, he could have walked away with the mayor's job. He gave the crowd a big *okay* sign and flashed a giant smile, and I coulda sworn his teeth shined like stars.

We darted out of the theater in front of the crowd and made our way backstage.

Rainy slumped in his chair. Beads of sweat dribbled from his scalp, ran down his face, and fell from his nose and chin.

Sweat-soaked clothes clung to his body. It never dawned on me that joking might be hard work.

He wiped the black from his face, constantly glancing into the mirror, like he was relieved that his reflection was still there. We told him what a great show it was. He smiled and said, "Thanks. I work theaters all over the place. Look me up any time."

He gave us two quarters each and let us sleep in his car.

The next morning, we split a doughnut and a cup of coffee at a diner. I gulped down my share and went to buy a pencil and a postcard.

Dear Mom, I wrote, *I am fine. How are you?*

I didn't tell her the bad things that had happened to me, and I argued with myself about putting something in about missing her, deciding against it because she probably knew it anyway. I promised to bring Little Bill home soon. I ended it with "Love, Collie," because, sappy or not, I figured she'd like to hear it. I dropped the card into a mailbox and met up with Ike to go out to the rails, where we jumped a lumbering westbound freight.

The wildest part of my search for Little Bill began.

We lay sprawled on the catwalk. I stared up at the empty sky. The freight snaked through hills and hollows covered in scrub brush and spindly pines. A few houses drifted past, shacks really, weather-beaten and shabby with a wobbly cow or stunted pig standing in the front yard.

I said, "Let's get into the boxcar."

"It smells down there," Ike mumbled.

"Smells?" I said, my voice rising in disbelief. "We've ridden boxcars that smelled like cat pee, like wet dog, like horse flop. Geez, we probably smell as bad."

He shrugged.

The train followed a sweeping curve around the base of a large hill that towered above us.

"Hey, a tunnel!" I chirped. I'd never been through one before.

"Geez! Get down!" Ike screamed.

"Huh?'

"*Lay flat!*"

I threw myself to the catwalk, as Ike shouted, "Hang on! Bury your face! Keep your eyes closed!"

The locomotive's black smoke, trapped inside the tunnel, exploded from its entrance like a cannon blast. It swept over me in a boiling, swirling cloud. I buried my face in my armpit. Hot cinders burned my hands, neck, and ears. I dug deeper into my arm. Then, suddenly, the choking, burning smoke disappeared, and we were in the clear. I coughed, rubbed my eyes, and wiped my nose on my sleeves. Ike scurried over on his hands and knees, and brushed my head.

"Your hair was on fire," he explained.

"Am I out?"

"Yeah. You want to go down now?"

"Yeah."

We wiped soot from our skin and clothes, until the train

stopped for water, and an old hobo swung into our car. The old codger had been on the road for years and knew all the lines. I asked about routes west to Denver.

He stroked his beard and said, "Getting to Denver? Y'all on the right path. This here feeder line will take you clear across Arkansas. Then you could jump a freight, take you across Oklahoma. But for my money, I'd swing up to Kansas and ride the Rock Island Line. Hell of a line, them boys know how to run a railroad. Once you hit western Kansas or Oklahoma, just about any train you jump will connect with Denver. Yup, you boys are doing okay."

Hunger was gnawing at us, so we hopped off at the first chance to scrounge for food. The town was small and worn down by hard times, but the people were kind, and we managed to collect something for a mulligan stew pot. We found the jungle beside a brook, and with it, several dozen young guys, and three bubbling stew pots, each attracting its own circle of worshippers. Ike reached into his pockets for the carrots and potatoes we'd begged and started to put them into one of the pots when a boy grunted, "Ferget it."

The kid, a big redhead with a lump-of-clay face, shot Ike a nasty look, and said, "Don't want no darkie's food mixin' with ours."

The others around the pot added their scowls to his.

With a tilt of his head, Ike led us away.

"We don't have to take his guff," I said.

"Yeah, we do. Don't be a dope. Look around," he said.

It took me a moment to understand. Ike was the only colored kid there.

We tried the next pot, but a sharp "beat it!" chased us away there, too. The hobos around the third pot grimly shook their heads as we approached.

We trudged to the far edge of the jungle. I fell onto some soft weeds.

"Get up. Find wood," Ike said.

"What's up?" I asked.

"Just look for wood," he said gently.

He made a campfire. Next to the blaze, he placed hand-sized stones he'd found near the brook. Taking the grub out, he divided the carrots between us and placed the potatoes on the hot rocks. We ate the carrots as the potatoes cooked. He turned them to keep their sides from burning. They were perfectly done when he'd finished.

I bit off small hot, hot pieces of the potato. There was no butter, no salt, no pepper, no *nothing* to put on it, but it was delicious.

"**T**own folks gave us food easy enough yesterday. Don't know when we're gonna get as good a chance again," Ike said the next morning. We decided to collect as much food and cash as we could before jumping a freight out of town.

We trudged down a street of small, sad houses that

hadn't seen fresh paint in a long time. We tried hitting up the owners for odd jobs, but our luck had turned and we kept striking out. Hours passed. Our stomachs were a chorus of grumbling. My feet ached and the sun squeezed a steady leak of sweat from me. Ike didn't look any better off.

"What smells?" I asked, picking up a sour odor.

"You do, ya dope," Ike grumbled.

I stuck my nose into my armpit. Ike was right. I stunk. I leaned toward him and took a whiff. Wrinkling my nose, I said, "You ain't no bed of roses either."

He shrugged and glanced at the sun, saying, "Can't remember the last time it rained."

I realized I hadn't seen a drop since I'd left home. Everywhere I'd been was bone-dry and dust-covered.

I went up to another house as Ike waited on the street. Going alone was a habit I'd kept from my time with Scarecrow, and I felt I had the knack to get jobs.

A woman answered, took one look at me, frowned, and slammed the door in my face. I plodded back to Ike.

"Geez, that was fast! What did ya say anyway?" he asked with a frown.

"Nothing. One look at me and, *blam*, that was that," I said.

"Musta said something, or she wouldn't have slammed the door."

Angrily, I said, "You wanna try the next one, big shot?"

He shrugged.

I tried again at another house, and an old man answered.

He had pipe cleaner arms, parakeet eyes, and he was tiny, a good head shorter than me. I don't know how somebody shorter could look down his nose, but he did. Still, I was able to cut a deal.

"Rugs need beatin'," I explained to Ike.

"Whadaya hit him up for?"

"A buck!"

"For how many rugs?"

I shrugged.

"You dunno? He might have a couple of dozen rugs to smack dust out of. An old coot like that probably expects us to work for days for a stinking buck!" he cried.

I said, "The house isn't that big. I figured—"

"You figured? What the hell do you know? Idiot. If it wasn't for me, you'd be stuck back with Papa Bear squeezing lemons until your fingers fell off."

"Whadaya talking about? It was me who led us out of there!"

"Yeah, after you blew a couple of chances to get away, ya dope!"

"Quit callin' me a dope. I'm sick of it. It's me who's sweet-talked us into the jobs. Ya know nobody woulda hired you, you . . ."

"What? You *what*?"

"Ah, shut up!"

"*You what*? Say it!"

"I wasn't gonna say anything!"

Yes you were. *Say it!*"

He shoved me.

The sting of it froze me for a moment. Ike glared at me. I hit him with my right hand.

But it was a wide-swinging sissy-punch, and it bounced off his shoulder. Still, it stunned him and I hit him again with my left hand in the chest. He stumbled backwards to the ground and I jumped him. We wrestled in the gutter, trading turns on top and slapping punches. I took a clean shot to my kisser and tasted blood. My hand went to his ear and I yanked a scream out of him.

A blast of water nearly had us jumping out of our skins.

The small man, seeing our fight, had dragged out a garden hose and soaked us. He yelled, "Stop it, ya hear! Where da ya think you are, the circus?"

We picked ourselves up and shot each other nasty looks.

"You gonna do my rugs or what?" the man asked.

He had four rugs to clean. We hung them over a line and smacked them with a wooden rug beater. At first, I imagined the rug was Ike, but after an hour of swinging the beater, the rug was just a rug.

Clouds of dust came off each of those four rugs, and by the time we finished, all of it seemed to have found its way to our wet clothes and skin, sticking to us like honey. The man said we couldn't use his garden hose to wash, but we did anyway after he disappeared back into his house. Then we snuck off, dripping.

"Ya don't stink anymore," Ike said.

"You neither," I said.

The next night found Ike and me on a catwalk under the moonlight. Four other young guys were up there, too. They were on their way to pick beans for twenty-five cents an hour. At least that's what they'd heard farmers were paying up the line. Three of them sat, while the last stood, a canvas bundle holding all his things tied in a *U* over one shoulder. His knees bounced to the jigs and jolts of the rumbling freight. He chewed gum.

"Sit down, Louie, why don't ya?" one said. "Whadaya think ya doing?"

"This is good practice. Helps my balance. For my next bout," Louie said.

"Next bout? What a moron," his pal muttered. Turning to Ike and me, he explained, "Last month, our string had run out. No money, no food. Nothing. Then we see where ya can make five bucks for boxing the local pro. Five bucks for just stepping into the ring with the mug, a bantamweight. Louie there is the only one to fit the bill, being the right weight and all, so we throw him up for the job."

"I was the only killer in the bunch, is the real reason," Louie added.

"Yeah, yeah. Ya gotta understand, Louie never punched nothing in his whole life except me, and that was when we was in short pants in the first grade. So our plan is for Louie to get into the ring, take a dive, and, *bingo*, collect the fiver.

Then we'd head to the nearest cafeteria and chow down on Swiss-steak dinners," the pal said.

"I thought it was spaghetti and meatballs," Louie interrupted.

"Steak, spaghetti, who cares? The thing was that we had a plan to take the money and run. The night of the fight arrives, the arena's filled, there's cheering and bright lights. Excitement, ya understand? Louie's head swells, and he decides he could take the guy!" the pal explained.

"Maybe I'd get a shot at the title," Louie said.

"Shaddup. Anyway, Louie puts up the old dukes and goes out and boxes the guy," the pal said.

"What happened?" I asked.

"Had the snot beat out of him! Later, the three of us are eating Swiss steak and Louie is sipping soup through a straw because his kisser is so swollen," he said.

"Lucky punch," Louie said, still standing.

"One punch could be a lucky punch. Twelve, fifteen punches means you're just a palooka," the pal said, and we all laughed, including Louie.

The freight suddenly slowed.

"Hey, what's going on?" Ike asked.

The front cars were pulling away from us. The coupling that attached our car to its front neighbor had somehow come undone. We were being left behind! A large gap grew between our part of the freight and the front end.

The engineer must have felt the load lighten on the locomotive and figured out the problem. He touched the brakes and the front end slowed rapidly. But our end didn't have brakes and we kept barreling along until we slammed into the front.

The crash sent Louie flying. I threw out a hand to grab him as he hurtled past but missed. He flew off the boxcar and disappeared into the night.

The train stopped not long after. Not for Louie, but for the engineer and brakeman to check the couplings. Louie's pals climbed down and talked to the railroad men. Me and Ike watched them in the light of the brakeman's lantern. The railroad men shook their heads at Louie's story, but continued down the boxcar line. Louie's pals headed down the rails, also, to look for their buddy.

Me and Ike could have joined the search, but I didn't really want to find what was left of Louie and I don't think Ike did either. An hour later, we were rolling again. Without Louie and his pals.

Hungry, we swung off the freight at the next town, where Ike put the bum on a well-dressed guy in a colored diner. Slipping in beside him at the counter, he asked the waitress, "Ya got any stale biscuits? I haven't eaten in days."

Just as Ike had hoped, the swell gave him the once-over, felt bad for him, and told the waitress to put an extra biscuit for Ike on his bill. Ike thanked him and ran out to share it with me. Later, we washed windows for a quarter and used the money for a sandwich. Our stomachs filled, we went back to the rails and caught one right away.

We joined a mob of hobos. The boxcar we jumped already had more than a dozen guys in it. Even with the doors open, it stunk to high heaven. We climbed to the catwalk and staked a place there among a bunch of others.

The locomotive got up a good head of steam, and we started high-balling along. The freight barreled through curves, making the boxcars tilt. Sparks flew from the screaming metal wheels.

"Yahoo!" somebody yelled, and we all joined in.

But soon after, the train slowed to a dog trot.

"Ah, crud," somebody muttered, which summed up all our feelings.

There was no breeze, and the hot sun beat down on us. More hobos joined us on the catwalk to escape the steamy boxcar. Everyone squirmed around to make room, and things got cramped. We all glowed with sweat.

The train rolled toward a town. I spied men lining the tracks and thought they were more hobos waiting to catchon. But as we neared, I saw they were bulls and coppers. It was too late to hop off and beat it. My heart jumped into my throat.

"Whadaya think?" I asked.

Ike shook his head.

The train kept rattling along.

"Wouldn't we be stopping if they were gonna grab us?"

Ike shrugged.

The bulls and coppers held clubs and revolvers. I saw a few shotguns, too, and even a bullwhip. The men glared at us as we slowly passed.

"Don't even *think* about getting off!" a bull shouted, patting his club.

"Stay out of this town," another warned.

"Keep going!" growled another.

"Heck of a welcoming party," a hobo joked. We giggled.

"I seen it before," said a guy sitting next to me. "Some towns think we're all crooks and mugs who just want to make a mess of their place. So they greet the freights and make sure nobody gets off."

"Lousy bums!" shouted the bull.

A hobo chucked an apple core, and the bull had to dance to dodge it.

"Stinkin' bull!" I screamed back.

Others chimed in. Soon everyone was chanting, "Stinking bulls! Stinking bulls!"

We shook our fists at them and they did the same back. Ike dropped his slacks and waved his fanny at them. We cheered.

A bull swung his shotgun toward us. Everybody ducked, and we kept our yaps sealed until we left the bulls and coppers far behind. But they stayed in our minds. Later, when the freight stopped, we all jumped up and looked for a bull ambush. We breathed easier when we saw no one coming for us. In fact, there wasn't *anyone* around. We were in the middle of nowhere.

A weak, hot breeze barely stirred the sand that sur-rounded us.

"This a desert or something?" Ike wondered.

"You don't find houses and barns in a desert," I said and pointed out a couple of them near the locomotive.

"Looks empty," Ike said.

Slats fell from their sides. Broken sticks that were once fence posts faintly outlined a once-upon-a-time yard. Here and there nibs of dead wheat stalks peeked through the sand. It all seemed haunted.

"Creepy," I said, and Ike nodded.

The train sat and sat. A few hobos said they'd ridden freights that sat on the rails for days.

"Days? I don't want to be here *days*," I said.

Me and Ike joined other hobos and climbed off the train to stretch out in the shade of one of the boxcars. There was nothing to eat, nothing to do, and nowhere to go. We napped.

I dreamed Little Bill had wrestled me to the ground and twisted me all up, but somehow I switched everything and dreamed of flattening him to the dirt and bending his arm.

"Uncle!" he shouted, and the dream ended

Scorching heat woke me. Woke Ike, too. As we straight-ened our legs, Ike dug his hands into his pants and cried, "A lousy jerk picked our pockets!"

We'd been robbed!

I thought about the town that didn't want crooked hobos around. Maybe they'd been right after all?

We spun around, stupidly hoping to see the pickpocket skulking away. But we were alone. Everyone else was standing on the stalled boxcars, pointing off into the horizon.

Me and Ike climbed on top of the car and soon discovered that getting robbed was the least of our problems.

"**I**t looks like the end of the world is coming," someone said.

The horizon had grown an uneven, dark band.

"What's that?" I asked.

The band grew larger, darker, and seemed to bubble.

"The craziest mirage I've ever seen," Ike said.

"I don't think it's a mirage," I replied.

"What is it?" somebody asked.

The horizon boiled now.

"A storm?" Ike said.

"I've never seen a storm like that before," I said.

Blue-gray clouds heaved upwards, churning and boiling, swallowing the sky until they loomed over us. Flocks of screaming birds passed us. Rabbits followed, racing away from the clouds.

"Lord, look at that," Ike whispered, pointing to a string of barbed wire curled from a broken fence post in the sand. The points of the barbed wire were glowing.

Crackling flashes of light exploded around us, like tiny bolts of lightning. A sour stink—electricity?—filled our noses.

A sudden blast of wind nearly blew us all off the top of the boxcar. Driving sand scratched my eyes, and I coughed hard. I couldn't see. I couldn't breathe.

"Get inside!" I shouted.

Climbing off the boxcar was a crazy, blind-man's-bluff free-for-all race to the ladders. People shoved and pushed wildly. I crawled along the boxcar edge and tried not to fall. I got to the ladder. People stepped on my hands and head as I climbed down. At the bottom, I kept hold of the boxcar, knowing if I lost touch, I'd never be able to find my way back. Bodies pushed me. The boxcar opening! I climbed in and squirmed to one side.

"Shut the doors!" someone shouted, and I heard them close.

I opened my eyes. The boxcar was nearly black. A gloomy mist of sand-filled air made everything seem dreamy and ghost-like. I didn't see Ike. The wind pushed sand through cracks into the car.

"It's coming through the slats!" I yelled.

We crumpled sheets of old newspapers, clothes, caps, *anything* to plug up cracks.

But the sand kept seeping into the boxcar, and hung in the air like a cloud. I buried my face in my arm. Howling wind rocked the car. An enormous gust punched the side of the car, tipping us.

"We're going over!" a voice screamed.

But we crashed back to the rails.

A side slat broke and sand by the bucketful flew through

the opening. I felt it pile up around my legs. My eyes were clamped tight against the driving sand, and I flailed blindly at the sand drifting around me. It covered my ankles and swam around my knees like a rising river. It was burying me!

Then the wind stopped, like a switch had been thrown to *off*. I peeked out. Everyone was shaking the sand from themselves like wet dogs drying. We waded out of the deep, fine sand toward the opened doors. Tears from our scratchy eyes left streaks across filthy cheeks. A brownish haze was hanging in the air, and it made me cough and sneeze. We climbed down from the boxcar and milled aimlessly. Ike found me.

"Geez, what was *that*?" I asked.

"Dust storm. They been a'coming and a'coming. Killing farms. Driving everybody off the land," said a nearby hobo.

The engineer and brakeman walked past, checking the cars and couplings. The engineer shouted, "Anybody hurt? Everybody in one piece?"

A couple of hobos had been blown off a boxcar and broke their arms. The railroad men tied their arms up in slings. Their kindness surprised me. The train began rolling again, We swept sand from the boxcars with the sides of our shoes and boots.

By nightfall, we arrived at a rail yard and a large town. There weren't any bulls or coppers to keep us on the train, so most hopped off. We trudged away from the freight, covered in dirt and dust, looking like an army of walking dead men.

Ike and me had no food, no money, and angling for work or food failed. We followed a side street in hopes of changing our luck, but instead of finding work, we found the Big Heart Mission and Soup Kitchen.

Seeing that made me want to cheese it. I turned away, but Ike grabbed my shirt, saying, "Hold it. We're hungry and beat. They'll take us in."

"The mission! Haven't we had enough trouble with missions?" I sputtered.

"Just that one—"

"Yeah, that one, and they're probably still looking for us. Maybe these guys are in cahoots with them—"

"Are you looney? Whadaya think, the missions send messages back and forth across the country? 'Be on the lookout! Two no-account hobo kids have high-tailed it from Missouri and are headed west! All alert!' Geez, Collie, you think they're like the FBI and we're John Dillinger?"

I felt kinda stupid when he put it that way, and I followed him into the mission. Even so, I slouched down and hid my face when we entered.

It was a big place, clean, and ran like a clock. Right off, we met a mission worker who sized us up and said, "Lice."

The name-calling steamed me until I realized he'd meant we *had* lice. We were ordered into the showers. He had our clothes washed, too.

Afterwards, we joined a soup line and got bowls that were filled with chicken, carrots, turnips, and potatoes swimming in a thick broth. Ike and me looked at each other and smiled.

But just like at Papa Bear's, the cost of the free meal was having to sit through a sermon. The fella who gave it was a small guy with a bald head as pinkish-white as a fish's belly. He spoke in a soft voice and plucked at his bow tie the whole time. He told us we'd find eternal shelter with the Lord. Most everyone fell asleep.

When he finished, we were taken to a giant room where we'd spend the night. No sleeping on the floor here. There were cots for all. I fell off right away and slept like a baby until morning. Breakfast was scambled eggs!

"This place got Papa Bear's beat by a mile," Ike said.

"Yeah. And I don't see any kids being forced to work here to beat a county lockup," I said.

We waited our turn for breakfast. Mission people handed out eggs, toast, and coffee. People carried away the food with giant grins plastered across their faces. One of them was an older guy, gray and skinny, a bundle of sticks and twigs.

Like a scarecow.

Scarecrow never spotted us. I made sure we dodged him and led Ike to a far corner. Scarecrow's and Ike's hair would have gone up if they'd eyed each other, and I didn't see the profit in that. It made me feel like I was doing something wrong by each of them for not standing for either of them.

Scarecrow had shown me the ropes of jumping trains

and the hobo ways, and I owed him something for it. But Ike had become my fast pal, and we'd stuck together through thick and thin, and I owed him plenty, too.

After breakfast, the mission shooed us out the door. Me and Ike ended up in a crowd of hobos waiting beside the tracks outside the rail yard, where boxcars were being joined together. We planned on hopping the freight when it got rolling.

But midday arrived and we were still waiting.

"Doesn't look like they're in any hurry moving that freight," I said.

"Bunch of loafers, them railroad guys," Ike said. "You hungry?"

I nodded. My stomach rumbled. Our egg breakfast was hours ago.

Ike said, "Let's go back to town and angle for food."

"Dunno. We could miss the train," I said.

"I think we got the time. It doesn't look like those railroad guys are doing a thing. Bet they've stopped to eat. I bet we got plenty of time to sweep a floor or clean windows, and earn enough for a roll or something."

"Really don't want to miss the train." I said. Then my stomach did another empty somersault, and I said, "Geez, let's go!"

We stopped next at a five-and-dime, a hardware store, and a feed store looking for odd jobs. But all we got was the high hat or cursed.

"Let's try the bakery," Ike said.

The old lady behind the counter was bent like a question mark and, by the looks of her sunken cheeks, shy of most of her teeth. Still, she had a bright smile for us. We asked if she could spare a roll or biscuit.

"Oh, it's too early for stale goods. Try later, hon," she said cheerily.

"Not gonna be here later, ma'am," I said.

I guess we looked like a couple of sad sacks because she gave us a fresh biscuit for nothing anyway. Tearing it in two, we sat down on the curb. But before we could eat, we heard the high ball—two short blasts of the locomotive's whistle—the signal it was about to leave.

"Geez! I told you we shouldn't have taken off!" I cried.

"Aww, we ain't gonna miss it. Got plenty of time to get back. Come on!" Ike said, and raced away.

The engine's smoke trailed across the sky, as it left the yard. The thought of another detour, dead end, or delay made me mad.

Reading my mind, Ike yelled, "It's pulling a long tail of cars. We got time."

We raced past the yard to its outskirts—neither of us wanted to risk the yard and the bulls. We caught up to the train and sprinted over the cinders. Ike pointed to an open door, and laughed, "There! Told ya we'd make it!"

He grabbed the door frame and threw himself in. I ran up to it and did the same, and clumsily tumbled into the car.

"Guess you were right!" I said, getting to my feet.

Before me, Ike and Scarecrow stood, glaring.

Scarecrow grunted at Ike, "Move on, boy. Don't want you here."

Ike didn't budge an inch. He said, "Just because a bundle of twigs in pants says 'jump' doesn't mean I have to. I got as much–"

Before he could finish, Scarecrow saw me. Wide-eyed, he exclaimed, "Pup? That you? Never thought I'd see you again. Watched the bulls take you away and said to myself, 'That's the end of ol' Pup.' But I was wrong, wasn't I? Where you been?"

He stuck out his hand. I kept my to my side and edged toward Ike.

"Got locked up. Escaped. Jumped trains. Making my way west. With my buddy," I said, tilting my head toward Ike.

"Your buddy? Him? You're pulling my leg!" Scarecrow exclaimed.

Shaking my head, I said, "Me and him been all over."

"Ya can't be pals with a darkie. You'll see, he'll do ya in, steal from ya—"

Ike barked, "The only thief here is you! Saw you steal my socks. Saw you clear as day. Saw you stuff 'em in your pocket!"

Scarecrow sneered and turned to me, saying, "That's what he told you, that I stole from him? And you believed him? Darkies lie all the time, Pup. You don't know them the way I do—"

"You don't know *nothing*!" I cried. "Him and me been through plenty!"

"You taking his side? After all I done for you. Weren't for me showing you hobo tricks, you wouldn't have lasted two days on the road. Weren't for me, you would have ended up in two pieces on the rail bed," Scarecrow growled.

"The way I figure it, we're even. Found you work and food, and you did a lot better with me than you could have ever done on your own. Kept you from a beating. I figure I paid you back, double!"

"The hell with you, ya miserable ingrate. Stick with the jig, if you're that stupid! Get the hell out of my car!" he grunted.

I said, "We're staying. If there's any leaving to be done, it'll be by you,"

Me and Ike stood shoulder to shoulder and stared at Scarecrow until he muttered, "Darkies and darkie lovers. Good riddance."

He snatched up his kit and threw it out the door of the slow-moving boxcar. After giving us an evil glance, he hopped out of the car. We watched him gather his stuff and climb into another car far down the line.

"Old coot!" Ike said.

Breathing easier, we hung our feet out the door and finally ate our biscuit.

The train wheels clacked, and I figured every click brought me closer to Little Bill.

"How long before we get to Colorado?" I asked.

"The way we're going now, when we're old, old men," Ike said.

The freight crawled, moving so slow that I could hop off, pee into a bush, and trot back to the car without a problem. For a while, me and Ike walked alongside the train to stretch our legs.

Even with both doors open, the boxcars were as stuffy as a closed closet. Riding the catwalk was worse. There wasn't even a hint of a shadow up there, and you'd cook in the sunlight like a piece of grilled meat. We found a tank car with small, flat decks over its couplings where we stretched out in the shade of a neighboring boxcar.

"Think this is Oklahoma?" I asked."Or eastern Colorado? Or Nebraska? Where'd we get on?"

"Forgot to ask."

The land around us was flat and brown all the way to the horizon, like a giant hand had ironed the wrinkles out of the earth, burning it in the process. The sky was blue. Where it touched the ground, flat white clouds were stacked like pancakes. If there were people, or houses, or towns, or cities out there, I couldn't see them.

The train jigged onto a siding next to the main rails and stopped. I swear I heard hobos up and down the freight moan at the delay. In twos, threes, and fours, they climbed from boxcars, tanker decks, and gondolas onto the cinders. People milled around or flopped down near the cinders. A few lucky stiffs pulled food from their kits. Me and Ike walked to a narrow dirt road that ran along the rails all the way to the horizon. Looking up and down, it proved there was nothing to be seen. We walked back to the train's shadow and sat.

A half-dozen colored boys walked toward the back of the train. They spied Ike and stopped.

"Y'all better head back. Nothing but trouble ahead," one said.

"Trouble?" Ike asked.

"Yeah. Town up ahead don't stand for no hobos or no colored folk. Especially no colored folk. Not even just passing through. Bulls give every freight the once-over. Find ya and grab ya. Beat you up a bit, and then hand you over to the police. And no short lockup. You get put on a road gang. Sixty, ninety days. Yeah. Trouble."

"Sez who?"

"Sez a couple of boys who know. They been picking all over. Been through the town lotsa times. Seen it with their own eyes."

"How come they never been grabbed?"

"They white. Nobody wants to grab them."

"White boys told you? How do you know they ain't pulling a fast one on you, playing you for suckers?"

"They seem straight to us."

"So on the word of these white boys you're gonna get off the train?"

"Just because they white don't mean they gotta be liars."

"But where are you going?"

"Walking back to the last town. This slowpoke train didn't take us very far. Figure we can walk it in five or six hours."

"You're nuts."

"Suit yourself. Just passing the word."

The boys walked off.

"I'll head back with you, if you want," I said.

"No sense in that. Your brother isn't far off. Why lose time by doubling back and searching around for another line?" he said.

"But those colored boys said—"

"What do they know? I bet that old Scarecrow had something to do with it, making up stories to scare them boys away."

"They said a couple of white boys told 'em."

"White boys, old Scarecrow, I don't care who said it."

"It's just, ya know, if you felt it would be better to go with those guys, I'd be okay."

"Better 'cause they're colored?"

"Better than sticking around—"

"With a white boy like you?"

"No. Better than taking a chance—"

"You're a dope, you know that?"

"Forget it!"

"I have!"

We were giving each other dirty looks when the boxcar started shaking like bacon in a fry pan. Both our faces widened in puzzlement.

A voice shouted, "The Express!"

A black speck appeared far down the line on the main track. The earth shook. A high pitched *weee-OOO* pricked our ears. I could make out a locomotive barreling toward us, its dirty smoke streaming back on the top of passenger cars. Steam blew low out of the engine, and hid the wheels. The rails hummed like a twanged fork.

WE-oooooo!

Everybody stepped back because, well, *because!*

The Express screamed past, rattling everything and everyone, and was gone in a heartbeat, leaving a swirling tail of wind in its wake.

"Holy cow!" someone gasped. We all cheered like the winning touchdown. Not long after, our freight began rolling off the siding and back onto the main rails. The Express had breezed past, and the path was clear again. The close call with the speeding passenger train kept us chattering. Nobody noticed that we were rolling into a rail yard and a mess of trouble.

Bulls appeared on both sides of the cars. A hobo leaped from a boxcar and dashed free. Another followed, escaping under the wheels of a train parked nearby.

"Geez, we gotta get outa here!" I said. We got ready to leap.

Blam!

The shotgun blast shook me nearly as hard as the

Express had. Like a couple of frightened rabbits, we backed away. The train stopped. Bulls stood near our doors. One held a club, the other a revolver. Shouts and curses flew. A bullwhip snapped. A young hobo cried. I pointed to the boxcar hatch. We climbed to the catwalk and lay flat. Others did the same, and we all hid.

The bulls had about a dozen hobos, kids really. They were made to turn out their pockets and spill their bindles. A bull poked his toe through the things, picking up the interesting ones, pocketing the valuable stuff.

"Hey!" yelled a captured hobo as a bull took his dollar. The bull clubbed him to the ground. Another hobo went to help and got boxed on the ears. He fell to his knees, cupping the side of his head.

Far ahead, two bulls dragged a tall, thin hobo by his armpits. One smacked his head with a flashlight.

Scarecrow!

"Nobody rides my train without a ticket! Ya hear that, 'bo?" he grunted as he swung the flashlight again and again.

The other bull broke open Scarecrow's suitcase and ground his things into the cinders.

Scarecrow pleaded, "Stop! Stop!"

They hauled him to his feet. A bull slapped him with the back of his hand. He raised his hands and muttered something to the bulls. They stopped. He pointed . . .

. . . to our boxcar!

One of the bulls cried, "Hey, we got a darkie back here!"

Scarecrow had ratted to the bulls about Ike!

A half dozen bulls surrounded the car. One yelled, "Come on down, boy!"

Me and Ike tried to crawl under the boxcar paint.

A bull climbed into the car and called out, "Hatch's open. Darkie's gotta be up on the catwalk."

"You don't want us to come there after you, boy. Best come down. It'll be easiest on us all," a bull warned.

Ike started to rise. I grabbed his shoulder and shook my head. He stood up anyway. I rose slowly with him.

"Climb down, boy," the bull ordered.

Suddenly, a fist-sized coal nugget streaked through the air and struck a bull in the shoulder. He cried out. More coal flew, and the bulls jumped for cover.

Hobos near the tender must have grabbed the black rocks and passed them around. Coal rained down while the bulls cussed and screamed.

I knew it wasn't for Ike. Heck, there were hobos who hated Ike for being colored as much as the bulls. And it wasn't for me. I was a stranger to them, just another hobo. They did it for themselves and to get even for every time a bull roughed 'em up, chased 'em off a freight, or treated 'em like dirt.

We had good arms and true aim. A bull got hit square in the kisser, and blood spurted from his nose. He dropped his club and stumbled away. Another bull limped away on an injured knee. Others dived for the safety beneath nearby boxcars.

Blam!

Buckshot sprayed through the wall of a neighboring box-car. The barrage of coal stopped. But the bulls were scattered helter-skelter, and everybody saw the chance to cheese it. We piled off the cars and raced for our lives.

It was lunatic. Hobos and bulls ran every which way. I bounced into a bull, knocking us both a bit senseless. Ike pulled me away before the surprised bull could grab me.

We jumped some rails and caught our breath behind a pile of ties before running to a lone boxcar. But a couple of bulls spotted us, and we leaped away again.

A bull grabbed Ike. He tried to twist free, but the bull didn't let go. I kicked the bull's knee. He howled and released Ike as he fell.

We heard the high-ball whistle. Twice. Two trains were leaving the yard. We spotted a long freight. Its coupling started banging as the locomotive pulled the slack of its long boxcar tail. We raced to it and threw ourselves into a boxcar.

Escaping gave us belly laughs—until a meaty hand appeared on the door, and a bull with a shotgun swung in. But his big belly and gun made for a clumsy catch-on, and he rolled onto the floor.

"You crummy rats!" he cursed, struggling to his feet and trying to draw on us with the shotgun.

We leaped out the other door.

Blam!

Buckshot flew out with us—but in a different direction. I hit the ground hard, and pain shot through my shoulder. Ike lay beside me glassy-eyed and breathless. The wind had been knocked from him, and I had to help him to his feet.

Blam!

The bull fired from the train, but he was a poor aim and it flew wild. We spied a passenger train leaving the yard. We started running for it, but Ike cried in pain. He'd twisted his leg in the fall.

He swung his arm around my neck, and I helped him hobble away. The bull raised his shotgun, but the train was in his line of fire. The knot in Ike's leg lessened, and he started running on his own power. The locomotive roared. We sprinted, and grabbed the handrails at the end door of the baggage car.

We were riding the blinds.

The power of the locomotive ran right into my hands. Vibrations in the handrail made me realize that we'd caught onto something very different from a lazy freight.

The train left the yards and gathered speed. Its whistle shrieked a warning down the tracks: "We're coming!"

Wind swirled around us. The ground flashed by. The car shook.

Who could have imagined such speed!

We speeded faster, and what was once a brisk breeze was now a storm. The locomotive thundered. The baggage car rocked hard. We tightened our grip. Bits of stone from the rail bed sprayed up and shredded our pant cuffs. Hot smoke from the engine whirled around our heads and burned our lungs. Hot cinders stung our face, arms, and hands.

Ike shifted his weight off his bad leg. My shoulder throbbed and my hands went numb. The roar of steam and speed made talk impossible.

Ike leaned against me and tried to rest his good leg. He grimaced. All my muscles ached from standing in one spot. My head pounded.

It seemed like we had been standing for ever.

I caught Ike's eyes closing and shook him. I wouldn't have been able to catch him if he'd fallen asleep and fallen. He mouthed "thanks."

More time passed. Another hour?

My head ached, and I could barely focus my eyes. My stomach felt like it was the size of a marble. We hadn't eaten in almost two days. I began to imagine we weren't moving at all, and that we were really being carried by hurricane winds of steam and smoke and dirt.

I lost track of time.

I awoke with a start. I'd fallen asleep. Ike had held on to me. I nodded and smiled weakly at him. Looking down, I saw a trough of water instead of a blur of rail ties. Was it a dream? Suddenly we were drenched in cascading water!

Ike pressed his mouth against my ear and shouted,

"The locomotive doesn't stop for water. Scoops it up on the fly!"

The water had washed over us in the process. We shivered in our wet clothes and the wailing wind.

Seven hours after we caught-on, the train finally slowed. We appeared to be nearing a city and a large station, but I was stumped to name it. The sun was setting. I realized we'd been hurtling east. East! Away from Little Bill!

The yard was busy. There were trains everywhere, their bells clanging and whistles screaming. We slowed to a crawl, but two freights, on either side of us, made it impossible to swing off. As we waited for our chance, the baggage door suddenly opened.

I thought they never opened, and nearly lost my footing in surprise. The mail agent who opened it was just as shocked to see us.

"Holy—" he called, and reached for the revolver strapped to his leg.

There was nowhere to hide, and the train still moved too fast to jump off. Ike and I could only lean away. The agent saw we were just kids and not train robbers. He holstered his gun and said, "You scared the bejesus out of me."

"Sorry, mister. We'll hop off first chance," I said.

The agent shook his head sadly at us and closed the door. Good to our word, when the train slowed to a trot, we swung to the cinders. But we were stupid with exhaustion and had only the strength to stand there as the train came to a stop.

"Hey, you!" a voice called.

A bull!

"Just come off the express, did ya?" he asked.

"No, sir," we lied.

"Don't try and pull a fast one on me. 'Course you came off that train. Filthy as rats. Well, boys, it's time to pay," he said.

I guessed paying meant being beaten, or taken to a local lockup, or both. I wished I had the strength to run.

"Sorry, chief, these characters belong to me," another voice said.

The mail agent.

"Like hell—" snarled the bull.

"'Fraid so, chief. It's federal. The mail and all. Trumps railroad detectives," said the agent.

The bull's eyes narrowed in fury.

The agent smiled and said, "Take a hike, chief."

The bull stalked off.

"Dope," the agent chuckled.

"You taking us to jail?" I asked and wondered what federal lockup would be like.

"Yeah, kid, you two *hombres* are gonna do hard time," he laughed.

Shortly afterward, we were chowing down on pot roast, potatoes, and string beans.

"**H**ell of a story, boys. You got something to tell your grandchildren," Jake said.

The mail agent, a middle-aged guy who reminded me

of the high school baseball coach, had told us his name.

Turning to the waitress, he said, "Pie all around."

After Jake had snatched us out of the bull's grip, he ordered us into a sedan with U.S. MAIL painted on the door, and drove us away. I was sure we'd fallen into hot water and was as low down as I'd ever been. But instead of ending up in a federal lockup, Jake bought us dinner at a restaurant near the yard. It was filled with men in overalls, and I would have bet they were all railroad men. Jake ordered us to a table where the waitress greeted him by name.

"Got yourself another couple of track orphans?" she asked.

He nodded, and asked, "What's good tonight?"

"I'd go with the pot roast," she said.

"Don't buck the advice of a waitress," Jake said, a good tip I'm gonna hold on to forever. The pot roast was swell!

Between mouthfuls of roast, we told him about Scarecrow, Papa Bear, Rainy Knight, the rails, the bulls, and Little Bill, of course. When we got to the part where we met him at the baggage car door, the waitress was setting down plates of blueberry pie.

Jake stabbed the pie with his fork, and said, "I guess after all you've been through, there's no stopping you now."

"Yeah. But the Flyer took us off in the wrong direction. I don't even know where we are," I said.

"Kansas City. But that's not too bad. Lines go direct to Denver. A freight can get you there lickety-split. Not as fast as riding the blinds, but I think you boys have had enough of that," Jake said.

Ike stopped eating pie long enough to say, "You said it, brother!"

After dinner, he drove us to a deserted corner of the rail yard where a lonely, battered caboose stood.

"Hasn't been in service for a while. You can spend the night there. Nobody will bother you. In the morning, there's a train leaving for Denver. It'll be flying a white flag with a red ball on the engine. Means it's a fast freight. You'll be shaking hands with Little Bill before you know it," he said.

We thanked him for saving us from the bull, for dinner, and for steering us the right way.

"Forget it," he said, and drove away. But not before stuffing a buck into each of our hands.

The caboose bunk was soft. I dreamed of me, Mom, and Little Bill being together. When I awoke in the morning, I figured the dream wasn't far off.

Not wanting to cross paths with any bulls, we awoke at dawn and waited for the freight just outside the yard. A crowd of hobos was there, and it was a mad rush for the cars when they rolled by. People crowded on everywhere—the rods, the ladders, inside the cars, on the gondolas, and on the catwalks. Ike and me went from boxcar to boxcar looking for a space, leaping the gap between catwalks.

My guts clenched the first time we did it. The train was going one way, we were jumping the other, and the earth was standing still. I glanced down through the couplings to the ties, blurry as they rushed beneath the train, and tried not to think about what would happen if I missed.

Finally, we found a spot to stretch out and enjoy the breeze. I started talking about getting to Denver and finding a train to jump to Little Bill's camp, when Ike gave me the bad news.

"I'm staying on," he said.

"Staying on? Whadaya talking about?" I asked.

"Heard this freight's headed to Seattle. I'm staying on and going through."

"But we're almost there. We just about made it."

"*You're* almost there. *You* almost made it. Don't get me wrong. I'm happy you're gonna finally catch up with your brother. But he's your brother, not mine. You guys are gonna pack up and head back to Wisconsin."

"But—"

"But what? I'm goin' back home with you? We gonna share a room or something? Or maybe you're gonna stay on the rails with me and we jump trains together from now until who-knows-when? Nah, that ain't gonna happen either."

"It's just . . ." I started but words stopped coming.

"Yeah, I know what you mean. But you don't owe me nothin'. And I don't owe you nothin'. We pulled for each other. We're even."

That was it. There was no arguing with Ike.

The sun shined but it didn't warm me.

The ride to Denver was straight through, and we never stopped. Finally we neared the yard and the time to jump off.

Me and Ike shook hands.

"See ya," we said to each other, just like it was the end of a school day and we'd be seeing each other the next morning.

"Ya know, for a dope who can barely swing an ax, you ain't half bad," Ike said.

"For a dope who can't swim, you ain't half bad either," I said.

I climbed down and swung to the cinders.

It was a sweet ride out of Denver. I rode an empty boxcar that smelled fruity, the leftover scent from its last load. The train moved at a crawl, struggling up a grade that followed the rising land. Mountains, *real* mountains with snow on their peaks, stood against the sky. I hung my feet out the box-car door and waited for my jump-off to arrive.

"Ya can't miss it," an old hobo had explained to me when I'd asked about the CCC camp. "There's a cattle spread right there. Got Canada Navy Chew painted across the barn wall. White on blue. Can't miss it. Big as life. Just follow the road there into the hills. It's not far."

Fair weather and the gentle rocking of the train made me drowsy. But the thought of sleeping right past Little Bill, after all the trouble I'd been through, kept my eyes open.

The train snaked through tall pines and rolling hills until we finally came to a couple of worn, wooden buildings. There wasn't a soul around. I barely made out AVY CHEW in faded red letters on one of them. It wasn't what the hobo said and I hung at the boxcar opening, not sure what to do.

"Geez, I hope this is it," I muttered to myself, and eased off the slow-moving train. Plunging into high grass that separated the rails from the road, I looked back at the freight as it disappeared and hoped I'd made the right choice. I followed the dirt road into the hills and through a dark and silent forest. An hour later, I was still walking. My legs ached from the climb and my throat was dry. Nobody and no camp were in sight.

"What a dope," I scolded myself for listening to the old hobo. I threw myself down onto a bed of pine needles. I laid flat and stared up into the treetops, resting before hiking back to the rails. Then I heard the truck.

It rumbled and rattled, its gears changing and grinding as the driver searched for the best way to coax the engine forward. I looked down the road and saw dust rise above the trees. I stood in the middle of the road and waited. The truck's large flat nose appeared first. It was a big logging truck with an empty load. I waved, and the driver stopped at my toes.

"Hop in, kid," he said without me asking.

The driver, a guy with a stubby beard, told me the camp was up the road about five miles. Explained he hauled lumber for a sawmill that bought downed trees from the camp. Explained he always picked up the CCC guys.

"My brother's at the camp. I'm not a CCC guy," I explained.

"Yeah, I was kinda wondering about you. Couldn't see a squirt like you swinging an ax. No offense, mind you," he said with a smile.

"Nah."

I was just happy for the ride.

He told me about driving heavy loads over little dirt roads. "A freaking nightmare," he said, but I was barely listening. The idea of finally reaching Little Bill made me squirm.

Rows of wooden buildings appeared in a clearing. Young guys were everywhere. It was what I'd imagined an army camp to look like, except with axes and saws instead of rifles. The truck stopped, and I hopped out. A bunch of guys tramped past me with axes slung over their shoulders.

"There's a *Moose* Collier," answered one when I asked about my brother. "Don't know his first name. His bunk is up there."

I trotted to the distant small building. Dashing up the wooden steps, I threw open the door. But instead of Little Bill, I found an empty room and two rows of cots. I sat on the steps and waited. Nobody paid me any mind. Young guys came and went, even squirts like me, and I guess people figured I was just one more.

As the sun dropped in the sky, a row of guys filed out of

the nearby woods. At their head was a large man holding an ax across the back of his neck with both hands. In the half-light, the dirt-covered man looked exactly like Dad.

Little Bill!

He saw me and froze. Then a smile sprouted on his face, and he raced to me, shouting "Collie!"

Hugging me quickly, he stared at me, surprise and shock flickering across his face like sunlight peeking in and out of the clouds. His buddies arrived, and he stuttered, "Hey, guys, this is my kid brother!"

Slaps on the shoulder and handshakes followed.

"Nice meeting ya, kid."

"How ya doing?"

"Ya never mentioned ya got a kid brother, Moose!"

"Whadaya talking about? I told you about him. Ed. *Collie*. He hates Ed," Little Bill said.

"Hey, kid, tell ya brudder not to be such a hump boss!" one guy said, and everyone laughed in agreement.

"Can it!" Little Bill said with a grin. His buddies drifted away and left us alone.

"Holy cow, Collie, how'd did you get here?" he asked.

"Jumped trains," I said.

"Like the hobos? Wow! A trucker friend of mine took me the whole way. Never thought to hop a freight. Too scary—"

"Let's go home, Little Bill!"

"What?"

"Mom's waiting for us!"

Little Bill's face darkened.

"I promised to bring you home. She really misses you," I said.

He avoided my eyes.

"Did you hear me? Mom wants you home—"

"I hurt her!" he cried in a cracking voice.

"That was an accident. She knows it. She forgives you." I touched his shoulder but he pulled away. "Mom wants you home. Wants us to be together. Wants you to be like Dad—"

"I am like Dad. Here. But I won't be back home!" he exclaimed.

"Sure you will—"

"*No!* I can't. I know that for certain!"

I shook my head in confusion.

"I meant to write. To explain things to Mom. And you. But it was *hard* to put it all down in black and white," he said.

"What was so hard?"

"Admitting I was no good at home. That I made a mess of things for you and her, that I made a mess of me! You know what I'm talking about. Fouling up jobs—"

"It was the Depression—"

"Guzzling beer. Getting drunk all the time. Hurting Mom—"

"But it looks like you straightened out—"

"I have! I don't drink at all, even when me and the guys get time off and we all head into town. I'm different here. I work hard. They made me the boss of my own gang. The guys look up to me. And the CCC people set it up so most of my pay will be sent home to Mom and you, so I know you two will be okay."

He held my shoulders.

"I'm different here, Collie. *Different.* Do you understand? I'm the way I think Dad would have wanted me to be. I think he would be proud of me now."

Looking into his eyes, I knew he was right. I'd seen it right off but was afraid to admit it because of all the trouble I'd had getting to him. But it wasn't about me and the past, it was about Little Bill and the future. Here in the forest, he'd found the right track. Taking him home would just throw him off the rails.

"Moose!" someone called. "We're gonna grab dinner. Bring your brother along."

"You hungry?" he asked, and I nodded. "The food ain't great, but there's plenty of it."

He hooked my neck with a crooked arm and pulled me close, holding me tight the whole way to dinner. I spent the night. Little Bill fixed that I could sleep in the bunk next to his.

The next morning, I tagged along with Little Bill and his crew as they cleared land to widen the camp and make room for more buildings. The guys axed small trees with thudding chops. The smell of raw wood, pine, and dirt filled the air. Trees fell with a splintery crack. Their branches, like outstretched arms, broke their tumble and muffled their crash to the ground. Little Bill hovered around the action, warning the fellas to keep their minds on the job as they teased each other with joking insults.

"Hey, Feldman, would ya believe me if I told ya my old mom can swing an ax better than you?" one asked.

"Murphy, I wouldn't believe you even *had* a mom," Feldman said, and everyone, including Murphy, laughed.

"All right, guys, let's keep the clucking to the henhouse," Little Bill said, smiling.

The last tree was the biggest, a thick thing I couldn't have wrapped my arms around. Little Bill looked at it, his ax swinging from his hand like a pendulum. He held out the ax to me and said, "Give it a shot."

I remembered the mess I'd made chopping wood with Ike. My arms stayed glued to my sides.

"Come on, take a whack," Little Bill said.

"Go ahead, kid," someone said.

"Yeah, take a swing," another voice called.

I took the ax. It was heavier than the one I'd used before, and I lifted it clumsily.

Little Bill said, "It's kinda like swinging a baseball bat, and you can do that, right? The only thing different is the big ax head. So you gotta start with one hand next to it, and then you let it slide down as you swing. Like this."

He stood beside the tree and swung the ax on a sweeping

path, half sideways, half downward, and buried the blade into the trunk with a drumming *thunk*. Pulling it free and handing to me, he said, "You can do it, Collie."

I planted my feet where his had been, reared back, and swung.

Thwack!

The hit wasn't as loud as Little Bill's, but it was hard enough to send a dinner-plate-size chip of wood somersaulting.

"Attaboy!" someone yelled, and the guys cheered.

Little Bill smiled and nodded. I whacked the tree again.

Thwack!

I hit it again and again until I had to stop to catch my breath and wipe the sweat from my hands. Little Bill took the ax from me, saying, "Let me finish 'er. Don't want this thing falling on you."

He threw his whole body into his swings. The ax flew in wide, sweeping arcs that drove the blade deep into the tree. After three strikes, the tree buckled with a gunshot crack and fell. Afterward, the guys sawed and chopped the fallen pieces. It didn't seem as much fun, and was like the difference between hunting a wild animal and butchering it.

Later, I ate dinner with the guys. They told me I should stick around and join the CCC.

"Nah, Moose's the only real lumberjack in the family. And I gotta get back and help my ma," I explained.

The next morning, Little Bill borrowed a car and drove me to a nearby town and rail line. In my shoe—for safekeeping—was money he'd saved, and in my pocket was a note to Mom I'd helped him write. He apologized to her and promised he'd return home as soon as he could. He wrote that I would explain the rest.

"I got to get back to camp. They expect me. Here, take this," he said, pushing extra dough into my hands. "Buy a train ticket. I don't like the idea of you jumping freights. It's too dangerous."

It was something a dad might say.

Behind me a whistle blew. Hissing steam sandpapered the air. Metal clacked on metal, and its vibrations found the soles of my shoes.

A train.

ABOUT THIS BOOK

Stories that made the greatest impression on me when I was growing up were those my parents and their contemporaries told of their own lives. Hanging between the twin poles of the Great Depression and the Second World War, their tales seemed to have a singular momentousness that fascinated me. They still do.

In *The Train Jumper*, I tried to capture the drama and spirit of the battered-but-undefeated America of the Thirties. In 1929, the value of securities sold on the New York Stock Exchange crashed. The economic version of a highway's multi-car pileup followed. Plummeting stock values forced bank closings, shuttered factories, and threw more than twelve million Americans, about a quarter of the workforce, off the job and into the unemployment line. The Great Depression had begun in 1929 and it battered America for about ten years. At its depth, an immense horde of mostly teenage boys and young men from all over the country took to the rails. Hopping on and off trains as if they were personal trolleys, they scoured the country for jobs and adventure.

Work was scarce and hard to come by. The drifters—hobos really—survived on seasonal agricultural work, picking beans, apples, and strawberries, for example, and odd jobs and handouts. Charity was as hit-or-miss as employment. Where some communities offered a helping hand and soup kitchens, others were aggressively hostile. Hunger was not unknown among the train jumpers.

It was risky travel. Just getting on and off a moving train put you in jeopardy of losing a limb or your life. Once aboard, a sudden lurch or jig could send you flying, or you could be struck by unnoticed tunnels, or snag a leg on bridgeworks and be dragged from an open door. Unsavory characters and thieves preyed on the inexperienced boys, too.

Railroads tried to stop the rail riding. Some of the guards, or bulls, were cruel, even murderous. They beat and robbed captured travelers or turned them over to the police, who, many times, treated the youngsters little better. Some bulls were less strict and merely chased people away. A few took pity on their forlorn prey and fed and housed them.

Pervasive racism, including segregation practices commonly known as Jim Crow Laws, made travel even more perilous for black drifters. In 1931, a group of African-American boys were taken off a Southern Railway freight near Scottsboro, Alabama, and falsely charged with attacking a white woman. The fate of the Scottsboro Boys is generally regarded as one of America's most glaring episodes of miscarried justice.

Regarding my use of the words "darkie" and "jig": painful as they are to hear, racial slurs were widely used at the time this story took place, in the 1930's, and to ignore them would have been historically dishonest. Commonly used racial epithets of the day were either detestable and despicable, or degrading and insulting. I chose to use the latter. "Colored" was a widely accepted description of race, even by African-Americans. The name of the venerable Civil Rights group, National Association for the Advancement of Colored People, or NAACP, reflects the then common usage of the word.

During the worst of the Depression, about a quarter million young boys, like Collie and Ike, and men rode the rails. American participation in the Second World War ended the widespread practice. Despite its many dangers and perils, for many who rode the rails, the screaming locomotives, rattling freights, crowded hobo jungles, and steaming mulligan stew became the lark of a lifetime and a vivid memory forever.

For those interested in more information, the book to read is *Riding the Rails: Teenagers on the Move during the Great Depression* by Errol Lincoln Uys. A film by the same name is a companion to the book and great fun to watch. The book and film inspired *The Train Jumper*, and I offer my heartfelt appreciation to both.

Studs Terkel's *Hard Times* is a terrific oral history of the Great Depression. The opening chapters of *The Glory and the Dream*, by William Manchester, offer a vivid portrait of America in the troubled 1930's. Russell Freedman works his dependably remarkable magic with *Children of the Great Depression*. The National Heritage Museum presents an interesting online exhibition, "Teenage Hobos of the Great Depression," at https://www.nationalheritagemuseum.org

Of course, the most vivid remembrances of the Great Depression are found on the lips of the man in the store, the woman down the block, your great aunt or grandfather. These people are the most precious of gems, those who lived history.